SHATTERED

HOSTAGE RESCUE TEAM SERIES

KAYLEA CROSS

SHATTERED

Copyright © 2017
by Kaylea Cross

* * * * *

Cover Art & Formatting by
<u>Sweet 'N Spicy Designs</u>

* * * * *

This book is a work of fiction. The names, characters, places, and incidents are products of the writer's imagination or have been used fictitiously and are not to be construed as real. Any resemblance to persons, living or dead, actual events, locales or organizations is entirely coincidental.

All rights reserved. With the exception of quotes used in reviews, this book may not be reproduced or used in whole or in part by any means existing without written permission from the author.

ISBN: 978-1979172332

Dedication

For Leann and Robyn, whose astounding individual courage and strength in the face of unimaginable fear and horror have earned my everlasting respect and admiration. This book is dedicated to them, their families and loved ones, and all others affected by the senseless tragedy of the recent mass shooting in Las Vegas as they begin the process of healing.

Kaylea xx

November, 2017

Author's Note

Dear readers,

I had every intention of diving right into DEA FAST book #5, but I've been itching to write a novella, and I missed my HRT guys so much, so…here we are. Hope you'll love the chance to hang with this crew for a while again. Get ready for an emotional rollercoaster as I bring you up to speed with everyone on the team.

Happy reading!

Kaylea Cross

Chapter One

"Got visual on target. Hundred-and-eighty yards and closing," Nate's team leader said quietly from the front passenger seat. His Alabama drawl gave the words an eerily relaxed feel that was completely at odds with the situation, but as a former Delta Force operative, pretty much nothing rattled Tuck.

Seated in the back between two of his teammates, FBI Special Agent Nate Schroder checked his weapon one last time, making sure the M4 was ready to go the moment they exited the moving vehicle.

His pulse accelerated, the rush of anticipation and adrenaline coursing through his body as addictive as the poison their target flooded the streets with. They rehearsed taking down vehicles all the time, but it had been a long time since they'd done a mobile assault in the field, and it was a total rush. He couldn't wait.

Their SUV sped through the darkened streets, moving to intercept their unsuspecting target ahead. West Englewood was one of Chicago's worst neighborhoods, riddled by poverty, crime and drugs. This time of night the streets were empty except for the dealers, users and hookers out on the street corners, looking for a sale or a fix.

By morning, more bodies would by lying in the county morgue, the latest casualties in the drug war that raged on these streets. The *Veneno* cartel's push to expand their supply within the U.S. had turned half of Chicago into a warzone, and the carnage showed no signs of slowing down.

Nate glanced at the screen mounted on the dashboard, the little red dot displaying their prey on the digital map. Only a few blocks separated them now, and the target had no idea they were coming.

The passenger in the suspect car was a wanted fugitive for a recent triple homicide in Miami, an undercover sting gone wrong that had resulted in the death of a twenty-six-year-old federal agent and the wounding of two others. Two arrest attempts had left three cops dead.

With all other options exhausted, the Bureau had called in Blue Team to arrest Raoul Sanchez.

After an ensuing sixteen-day FBI manhunt to find him and one lucky-ass tip yesterday morning, the hunt had come down to this moment. Except with the vehicle's darkly tinted windows, they weren't sure how many people were in the car. Could be two. Might be five. But however many there were, they were armed to the teeth and wouldn't surrender quietly.

Behind the wheel, Jake Evers kept his foot on the gas and his gaze locked on the road while team leader Tuck navigated as they closed in on their unsuspecting target, a shiny new black BMW. Another SUV holding their remaining three teammates was somewhere up ahead, coming at the target from the west via another street. They would converge in another four blocks, suddenly boxing the suspect vehicle between them and forcing it to stop a split second before the assault began.

"Vance, you ready?" Tuck asked the other vehicle's navigator via the radio.

"Roger," the familiar bass voice responded. "In position and waiting on your signal."

"Stand by." Tuck monitored the location of the BMW on screen while Nate and the others watched through the windshield, anticipating the moment they turned the corner and finally got a visual on the target.

Nate mentally counted down the seconds as they raced toward the next intersection.

Three. Two. One...

At the corner Evers turned a sharp right and accelerated smoothly without the squeal of tires to give them away. The Beemer was right there fifty yards ahead, its taillights glowing red in the darkness.

"Hit it," said Tuck.

A burst of adrenaline hit Nate's bloodstream as Evers floored it, the SUV speeding along the cracked, uneven asphalt in pursuit of their target. An FBI SWAT team and other agents were waiting a short distance away to assist and process the scene once the takedown happened.

But Nate and his boys didn't need backup for this. These sons of bitches were going down right here and now.

Tuck keyed the radio to contact Vance as the BMW picked up speed. "He sees us. Intercept now."

"Roger."

Nate gripped his weapon and angled his body toward the right rear door, ready to burst from the SUV the moment Blackwell threw the door open. His muscles tensed as the SUV carrying the rest of the team screamed around the next corner and barreled toward them.

The BMW's brakes slammed on with a satisfying squeal of rubber on asphalt.

Evers stomped on the brake, stopping a mere foot from the target's back bumper.

"Go," Tuck commanded.

Next to Nate, Blackwell threw the back door open. They were all out of the SUVs in the blink of an eye: seven big, well-trained men with their rifles up as they converged on the Beemer.

Before the occupants had time to react, Nate fired a 40mm gas round through the back window. It punched a hole through the glass and exploded, releasing a cloud of gas into the dark interior.

"FBI!" Tuck shouted, heading for the driver's door with Blackwell right behind him, and Nate moving to the rear door. The other team was responsible for taking down the passenger side. "Come out with your hands up!"

A split second later all four doors burst open, and a cacophony of gunfire split the night as the occupants unleashed a hail of fire at them. Nate dove onto his belly and returned fire as his teammates did the same.

Dozens of rounds hissed past him, impacting the asphalt and slamming into the front of the SUV. Nate ignored everything but the left rear door, his finger on the trigger.

A body fell out of the door. Nate locked on it instantly, caught the automatic weapon in the man's hand. Nate fired, hitting him in the chest. The guy grunted and fell, but didn't stay down.

Ballistic plates.

Nate aimed a fraction higher and fired again, this time striking the guy just below the collarbone. He fell with a cry that sounded over the gunfire, the weapon still in his hand.

Tuck was screaming commands at the suspects. Ordering them to put down their weapons and surrender. They'd been ordered to capture the wanted trafficker so the Bureau and DEA could question him before prosecution, but the HRT would take out every last one of these assholes if necessary, because the team's safety came first.

More bullets erupted from the BMW, and Nate's teammates returned fire. The second there was a lull in the firefight, Nate shot to his feet and stormed the vehicle with Tuck and two others.

Blackwell had already dragged away the guy Nate had shot and was busy cuffing him, so Nate reached into the backseat and grabbed the first thing he could reach—a meaty shoulder. He twisted his gloved fist in the perp's shirt, registered the hard strap of a ballistic vest before turning and wrenching the guy out of the vehicle with all his might.

The man hit the road with a thud and lost his grip on his pistol. It clattered along the asphalt but before he could grab it, Nate was on him. Nate slammed an elbow against the side of the asshole's head, didn't even pause before rolling him to his belly and straddling his lower body, pinning the thick arms behind the man's back.

"Fuck you, asshole," the guy spat, twisting and bucking under Nate's weight. As soon as the light from the streetlamp hit his face, Nate recognized the goateed and highly pissed-off face of their high value target, Raoul Sanchez. "I'll fucking kill you, *cabrón*," he growled, his dark eyes drilling into Nate's.

Yeah, not today, amigo. Or any other day for that matter.

Nate didn't bother responding aloud, clenching his jaw as he fought to hold the strong, enraged bastard still enough to get the flex cuffs around Sanchez's wrists while his teammates dealt with the other suspects.

Even when he had Sanchez's hands secured the asshole wouldn't stop fighting, animalistic roars of rage coming from him as he twisted and kicked in a useless effort to break free. A knee mashed into the nape of the neck solved that, with the added bonus of grinding the side of the asshole's head into the pavement. Sanchez went still and let out a scream of fury that seemed to echo off the crumbling facades of the buildings along the sidewalk.

Pinned and helpless. Defeated. And about to be thrown into federal prison for a damn long time.

Breathing fast but pumped after the victorious wrestling match and nabbing their HVT, Nate stayed right where he was and finally allowed his attention to stray by looking up. His teammates had four other men pinned and cuffed.

Bauer, the team's big man, had a guy almost his size pinned to the ground, his posture mirroring Nate's. He caught Nate's eye and a big grin split his face, the former SEAL in his freaking glory getting physical with a suspect.

"Who've we got here?" Tuck drawled as he came up next to Nate and aimed a tactical flashlight into the perp's face. Sanchez flinched and clamped his eyes shut, muttering threats and curses in Spanish. Tuck laid a hand on Nate's shoulder and squeezed. "Nice work, Doc."

"Hey, Doc. Need you over here."

Nate swung his gaze over to Blackwell, who knelt beside the perp Nate had shot. The man was stretched out on his back, the front of his shirt glistening in the faint light coming from the closest streetlamp. They all had combat medicine training, but as a former AFSOC Pararescue Jumper, Nate had been given the role of team medic, which he loved.

Tuck waved Nate away. "Go treat Sanchez's 2IC. I got this." As Nate eased to his feet, Tuck crouched down to plant a knee in the center of Sanchez's spine, holding him in place.

His 2IC? They definitely needed him to stay alive.

Nate hurried over and knelt beside Blackwell, who already had a pressure dressing on the wound in the man's upper chest, both hands stacked to help stem the bleeding.

The patient was unconscious from shock and blood loss, but still had a pulse, albeit weak. Someone dropped the medical bag onto the ground beside them.

"Paramedics should be on scene any minute," Vance said in his deep voice.

Nate nodded, tugging on his latex gloves. Sirens echoed in the distance, signaling the approach of the rest of the taskforce and medical personnel. But this perp needed help now, or he'd be dead before the ambulances arrived. "Anybody else critical?"

"Negative."

Nate got the large bore IV started in the patient's arm and pushed the volume expander into his system to buy time. The man had lost a lot of blood but his airway seemed clear, and there was no frothing or bubbling from the wound that would signify a hit to the lung.

Emergency personnel arrived a minute later, and the patient's vitals were steadier. He'd definitely make it to the operating table. It didn't matter to Nate whether a patient was a good guy or a bad one, he always did his best to save them, because that was his job and he took his professionalism seriously.

After handing off his patient to the EMTs, Nate stood and peeled off his bloody gloves. All the prisoners had been turned over to the newly arrived agents. Tuck was speaking with other members of the taskforce. Evers and Bauer were busy checking out the interior of the car, while Cruz and Vance checked the hood and Blackwell searched the trunk.

"Need a hand?" Nate asked.

"Yeah, start documenting all this," Bauer answered, emerging from the BMW with a sawed-off in hand.

Nate started filming everything and writing up a list. Within a few minutes they had a small pile of automatic weapons and ammo gathered on the ground, along with a bag full of cash and a couple kilos of coke.

"Okay, that's a wrap for us," Tuck said to them. "Forensics is taking over now. Good job tonight, boys."

The announcement was met with a lot of smiles and high-fives. They were going home to Virginia, and Nate couldn't get there fast enough. It had been way too damn long since he'd seen his little warrior.

He still couldn't believe how lucky he'd gotten to have Taya reappear so suddenly in his life.

With her calm, gentle nature she'd helped heal hidden wounds he'd been carrying around for years ever since that horrific day in Afghanistan when fate had placed her life in his hands. She made him a better man, owned him heart and soul, and he couldn't imagine ever living without her.

Chapter Two

Smothering an eye-watering yawn, Taya kept her fingers laced with Nathan's as he led her to the front door of his commander's house for the team gathering. The sexy half-smile he shot her sent a wave of warmth washing through her, but didn't erase the combination of excitement and anxiety fluttering in the pit of her belly.

She'd planned to tell him the news when she'd gotten home from San Francisco late last night, but the moment they'd walked into their condo he'd pounced on her, making it impossible to think at all, let alone talk. Afterward, she'd fallen straight into a deep, dreamless sleep that had kept her under until it was time to get ready to come here. She'd started to bring it up on the drive here, but he'd wound on the phone for the last half of it.

She couldn't wait much longer. He and the guys were leaving again tomorrow for another training thing down in Florida. So after the barbecue was over, she was going to tell him. She couldn't tell him one piece without the other, and his possible reaction to the first part kept making her hesitate.

Noticing her attempt to hide the yawn, Nathan raised a dark auburn eyebrow at her as they stepped up onto the front porch. "You gonna make it? You only slept what, twelve hours since you got home last night?"

Her lips curved at his teasing. "I'll do my best." The slight jetlag wasn't helping matters.

A baby's happy gurgle came from behind them on the street. Taya looked over her shoulder as Clay Bauer appeared at the foot of the brick walkway with his five-month old daughter in the crook of one muscular arm. Her heart squeezed at the sight. "Hey, you two. Where's Zoe?"

"She'll be here in a bit. Had to grab some stuff from the store." He shifted the strap of the diaper bag over his shoulder and loped up the steps to join them. "Okay, Miss Liberty, let's do this." Libby grinned up at him, her eyes locked on his with complete reverence.

Someone had their badass daddy wrapped securely around her little finger. Clay might be six-four and well over two hundred pounds, but one look at that baby's smile and every one of his harsh edges softened. It was too freaking adorable. Without a doubt Nathan would be exactly the same when his turn came.

Taya glanced at him as they entered the house, indecision warring with her normal common sense. Should she pull him aside and come clean right now? Maybe he wouldn't be upset about the first part. Then she could just tell him the rest and enjoy the evening.

Or he might be furious. She had a feeling he might.

Yeah, she'd wait until they left.

They all walked through the bright living room/kitchen together and out through the French doors that led onto the expansive wood deck outside. Shading her eyes, Taya took in the sight of Nathan's teammates and some of the significant others all gathered around the deck and yard. The scent of grilling meat made her mouth water. She'd slept so late she'd missed breakfast and lunch.

"Well, if it isn't Bauer and the Schroders," Commander Matt DeLuca said, adjusting the brim of his Chargers ball cap as he manned the grill. "'Bout time. We were starting to think you guys weren't coming."

Nathan tugged her toward his boss. "Yeah, I had trouble dragging someone out of bed because I guess I must have worn her out last night." His eyes gleamed at her with pure male pride.

"Too much information," Matt said, his attention on the grilling food.

"Way too much," Taya agreed, nudging Nathan with her elbow in warning.

"I've got a real excuse," Clay said. "Libby and I had a major diaper incident that required a type one hazmat response as we were getting into my truck. I had to take her back inside, throw out what she was wearing and hose her down. And now I so deserve a beer."

Matt cracked a laugh. "That sounds pretty bad."

"It was the shits."

Taya chuckled at Clay's wit. It was always a surprise, seeing someone as hard and serious as him cracking a joke. He'd sure warmed up a lot since Libby had come along, though his wife deserved most of the credit. Zoe was one of a kind, and a force to be reckoned with.

"Good to see it didn't damage your sense of humor," said Nathan.

Most people would say Clay didn't have one to damage, but then most people never got to know him the way they did.

Clay shrugged. "Good news is, she's empty for at least a day now." He aimed a proud grin at his daughter, who peered up at him with bright blue eyes identical to his own. "Zoe's on her way, she just had to stop and grab something else for the appetizer."

Matt waved his grill tongs at them. "You guys grab a drink and relax. Food'll be ready in two shakes."

"Sounds good to me," Nathan said, squeezing her hand.

She, Nathan and Clay took the wooden steps down to where the rest of the team and their ladies were either sitting on lawn chairs and chaises or standing around talking. "Hey," she said to everyone, glad to be part of such an amazing group of people. And even gladder for the distraction of her impending conversation with her husband.

A chorus of voices called back in greeting. Nathan let go of her hand to fish out his phone and take a picture of Clay and Libby gazing intently at each other. He examined his handiwork, a smug expression on his ruggedly handsome face. He was just so damn sexy, could still give her butterflies with a single look or touch. "This shot is just too awesome. Seeing you with her never gets old, man. Big, badass Bauer with a baby on his hip and carting around a diaper bag."

"Yeah? Well how about big, badass Bauer goes and gets himself a cold one while you hold the baby," Clay said, thrusting Libby at him.

Nathan's smile slipped and a hint of alarm crept into his hazel eyes, his hand frozen around the phone he was in the process of shoving back into his front jeans pocket. "Uh, well—"

"Here." Clay shoved Libby at him, didn't even try to hold back a grin as Nathan held her at arm's length with a look of pure panic on his face while he and Libby stared in astonishment at one another. "Be back in a few." He dropped the diaper bag on the grass next to Nathan's feet.

Taya couldn't help but laugh. "Oh, for crying out

loud, Nathan. You look like he just handed you a live grenade or something." It was pretty funny. He was great with kids, but babies apparently made him nervous. Well, it was time he got over it. "Give that precious angel to me." She held out her arms toward Libby, a big smile on her face. She loved babies, and they all spent enough time together that Libby knew her. It was impossible not to love the little sweetheart.

Instead of handing her over, Nathan cradled Libby closer. "No, it's okay. I'm good." Lowering himself onto a lawn chaise, he turned Libby around and sat her on his lap, her back resting against his wide, powerful chest. "I like your outfit, Libby."

Her little black onesie had a frog skeleton on the front and the words *My Dad Can Kick Your Dad's Ass* beneath it. Libby craned her head back to gaze up at Nathan, stared at him for a second, then grinned.

Taya swore her uterus swooned, the sight before her turning her entire body to mush. *God, I want to tell him.* It was tying her in knots. "Well since you two look so cozy, I'll go get us some drinks."

She headed back up onto the deck and grabbed an ice-cold bottle of Nathan's favorite beer from the cooler at Matt's feet just as his wife, Briar, sauntered out of the kitchen with a platter of sliced watermelon in her hands. Her face brightened when she saw Taya. "Hey, you came!"

The reaction touched Taya deeply. Briar was a true loner, which made a lot of sense considering her former role as a sniper—and from what Taya had heard she'd been every bit as deadly as her Marine Scout/Sniper husband. She had become more comfortable with gatherings like this over the past year or so, but seemed especially at ease with Taya.

Taya smiled at her, curbing the impulse to give her a hug. Hugs sometimes still made Briar a bit uncomfortable. "Hi. Can I help with anything?"

"No, Matt and I've got it under control." Briar's sharp, dark gaze did a sweep of the yard and stopped on Nathan and Libby. Her eyes widened. "Wow, will you look at that." She cocked her head a little as she watched them. "If I didn't know better, I'd think he kind of likes it."

"He does. It's so sweet I can hardly take it," Taya said, a tangle of emotions balling up in her chest. "I think he was just afraid of accidentally breaking her when she was first born, because he seems fine with holding her now."

Snagging a beer from the cooler, Clay shrugged and twisted off the cap. "Good, because I didn't give him a choice. You guys need a hand here?" he asked Briar and Matt.

"No, we're good. Go relax," Matt told him, catching his wife around the waist and hauling her in for a quick kiss. He got a playful, narrow-eyed look from Briar in return for the public display of affection that just made him grin.

After delivering Nathan's beer and with Libby safe in his capable hands, Taya and Clay went around to say hi to the others. Adam Blackwell and his wife Summer were off to one side, two-month-old baby Sam on his daddy's lap as they talked with Ethan Cruz and Marisol. From the way Soli was watching baby Sam with such undisguised yearning, Taya didn't think it would be too long until those two got hitched and started a family of their own.

And she completely understood that same yearning.

Sawyer Vance sauntered down from the deck wearing his trademark black Stetson. "Where's your better half?" Clay asked him.

"Carm's been at a medical tradeshow all week. Her plane should be landing in another hour or two. She's catching a shuttle home with her boss." He smiled at

Taya. "Heard you just got back from a road trip yourself."

"Yes, last night. It's good to be home."

"I hear ya. Coming home never gets old."

No, not when the person you loved most in the whole world was there waiting for you.

Clay tipped his beer to his mouth and took a long sip, eyeing Sawyer. "Heard Mama Cruz is coming into town tomorrow."

"Yep." A blindingly-white grin broke across his deep brown face.

Clay shook his head and smothered a laugh. "You're seriously the only guy I know who loves having his mother-in-law around all the time."

Sawyer shrugged. "Future mother-in-law," he corrected.

"They're sickening together," Ethan said, one arm draped around Marisol's shoulders. "Can't get enough of each other, always texting or talking on the phone."

"You're just jealous," Sawyer said with a smug grin.

"Dude, I'm *relieved*," Ethan corrected. "Means she always stays with you guys whenever she comes into town." He lowered his voice and waggled his eyebrows at Marisol. "Which means we get a lot of privacy."

"Oh, my God, Ethan," Marisol gasped, swatting him across the chest.

"What? It's true. And you love having privacy, because that way we can run around naked and do whatever we want wherever—"

Taya bit her lip to keep from laughing as Marisol clapped a hand over Ethan's mouth to stop whatever else he was going to say. Her cheeks were bright pink, her blue-green eyes shooting fire at him. "Honestly, I can't take him anywhere."

Ethan just chuckled and kissed her palm before tugging her hand away from his mouth. "No, for real, I'm happy she's coming up to help you guys with the wedding plans," he said to Sawyer.

"How long now?" Adam asked Sawyer, deftly shifting Sam to his other arm. Taya mentally shook her head. Watching these guys with their babies was enough to send any woman of childbearing age into instant ovulation.

"Little over four months," Sawyer answered, then leveled a hard look at Ethan and Marisol. "When are you guys gonna set a date, anyway?"

"Right after we see how things go with your wedding," Ethan answered without missing a beat. "Then we'll know if we should just go elope instead."

"You should totally elope," Matt called out from over by the grill. "So much easier, and cheaper. Right, honey?" he said to Briar.

"Oh, it's the *only* way to go," she answered.

Ethan raised his eyebrows at Sawyer, a gratified smile curving his lips. "They might be onto something."

Taya frowned at Marisol. "Would your families be okay with that?" They were a close-knit bunch, and pretty religious. Elopement didn't seem to fit with what Taya knew about them.

Soli shrugged. "Probably not. But I'm with Ethan on this one. We're in wait and see mode." Her eyes brimmed with laughter as she raised a bottle of hard cider to her lips.

"Oh, good, y'all didn't start eating without me."

They all turned at the sound of that familiar Louisiana-tinted female voice behind them. Zoe Bauer sailed through the French doors in her full Victorian Goth glory, bearing a tray of appies, a big grin on her shocking-red lips.

Today she had on a black ruffled Victorian-style skirt that was short in front, showing off her killer legs to above the knee, the back of it trailing out behind her in a short train. A bright purple corset-style top bearing the picture of a book with the words "Smart girls read romance" on the cover stretched taut across her chest. She'd dyed the top half of her hair a bright turquoise and left the long bottom layer black, and she had her trademark smoky eye shadow and liner on, making her amber eyes seem twice as bright.

Clay slung an arm around his wife's shoulders when she waltzed up to him in her bat wedge sandals. "Libby's not constipated anymore," he told her.

Those golden eyes locked with his, a smile lurking in their depths. "Oh?"

"We're down one dress, a onesie, and the car seat liner though. I couldn't save 'em."

Zoe laughed, that distinctive husky, dirty edge to it. She *was* a romantic horror author, so it suited her perfectly. "I see our daughter's already making the rounds." She nodded toward the yard, where Jake Evers and his girlfriend Rachel had Libby now.

Tuck was there with his wife Celida as well, all of them talking with Nathan. Once again, she marveled at her husband. Nathan drew people to him without even trying, his natural charisma pulling them in. "She's already turning into a party animal."

"Well, she's got to be a hangry party animal, so I'm going to feed her so we can avoid a meltdown. Hey, Taya. Good to see you." Zoe held out her arms expectantly.

Taya stepped into the hug, Zoe's floral-musk perfume wafting around her. She was the most physically affectionate person Taya had ever met, and it was always genuine. "You too. You look fantastic, by the way."

"Yeah, she does," Clay murmured, giving his wife a wolfish, approving look. With his arm around her he led her over to their daughter, Taya trailing behind them. The moment Libby saw Zoe, her eyes went wide and she twisted in Rachel's hold, arms reaching out, her expression desperate.

"There's my little raven," Zoe cooed, and scooped her from Rachel.

"Jeez, she didn't even try to be subtle about it," Rachel said with a laugh.

"Don't take it personally. I'm her only food source," Zoe joked. "And even still, I'm not her favorite human anyway. That's all daddy." She aimed a sidelong look at Clay, adoration clear in her gaze. "I swear she already thinks he hung the moon just for her."

At her words Taya shifted her gaze over to Nathan, who stared back at her with a smile so full of love it made her breath catch. Oh, man she wanted to drag him out to the truck and get it all off her chest.

"Wouldn't put it past him," Jake said with a smirk. "She's got him wound around her little finger so tight it's a wonder he can breathe."

"Can't help it," Clay said, smiling at his daughter, who was patting Zoe's face with her tiny hands. "When your little girl wants something, you give it to her."

"Are you gonna feed her, or can I have a turn holding her?" Celida asked, handing Tuck her drink before approaching them. She gave Libby a silly, open-mouthed smile that stretched the bullet scar on her right cheek, and the baby grinned back, delighted.

"She can wait a few minutes longer," Zoe said, handing her over.

While the women fussed and cooed over Libby, Taya sank into her husband's lap and draped her arms around his neck. "Hi," she breathed, leaning in for a kiss. The nerves were still there, but not as strong now. Even if he was mad about one of the things she told him, maybe his reaction to the other would smooth things over. She hoped it would.

"Hi." He slid his hand into the back of her hair, his warm, full lips lingering on hers. "You still tired?"

"A little, but I'm glad you dragged me out of bed for

this. I love it when we all get together." With the guys' intense training and ops schedule it didn't happen often, especially since she and a few of the other women traveled a lot for their own jobs. It was so nice to be together in a relaxed setting and spend time with the people who had become like family to her and Nathan.

"Hey, get a room if you're gonna do that kinda thing," Clay called out. "I got my young, impressionable daughter over here watching you two."

Taya flushed a little but Nathan only laughed. "You're just jealous because we're getting eight hours of sleep a night."

"I'm so damn jealous," Clay said, deadpan.

Zoe curled an arm around his waist and leaned her head on his chest. "Remember when we used to sleep that much?"

"Nope."

She looked up at him in surprise, then laughed when she caught his not-so-subtle meaning. "Ah, the good old days."

No. *These* were the best days, watching their daughter grow, and anyone who saw them would know it instantly. Taya couldn't wait to experience it firsthand with Nathan.

He ran a hand over her back. "You hungry?"

"Yes." And about to burst. How long until they left?

"You stay put. I'll grab us some grub."

"Okay." She finally got a turn to hold Libby, cuddling her and playing peek-a-boo, her heart squeezing when the baby let out a belly laugh.

"Here, trade you." Nathan handed her a loaded paper plate and scooped Libby up, making a silly face. The baby squealed and reached her tiny hands out to pat at his face, her expression turning to amazement when she rubbed over the dark bristle on his cheeks.

In that moment Taya fell in love with him all over

again, invisible fingers squeezing around her heart until her chest ached.
I have something I need to tell you…
For now, all she could do was wait.

Chapter Three

The sound of the hair dryer reached Sawyer Vance the moment he opened the apartment door, sending a burst of excitement through his veins.

Carm's home.

He'd left the barbecue as soon as manners would allow, right after wolfing down his meal, hoping to be here when Carm arrived. He would have picked her up but she had insisted he enjoy some downtime with his teammates. She'd managed to beat him home but if he was quick, he could still sneak into their bathroom and surprise her.

And if he was real lucky, she'd be naked.

He set his Stetson, wallet and keys on the kitchen table and strode to the master bathroom. Pushing open the door a few inches to a cloud of steam that puffed out into the hall, he caught sight of his woman and stopped short, desire roaring through his body.

With her back to him and the noise of the hair dryer, she hadn't yet realized he was there, giving him the opportunity to drink in the sight before him. Carmela was stark naked, all that long, dark hair curled over one shoulder as she dried it, exposing the line of her back, the indent of her waist flaring out to the swell of her hips and that sweet peach of an ass to his avid gaze.

His fingers itched to stroke all that smooth, golden skin and curl around those curvy hips. Damn, it had been way too long since he'd been inside her. Their jobs kept them apart a lot.

Stepping up behind Carm, he slid both arms around her waist.

"Oh!" She jerked her head up, her honey-gold eyes wide as they met his in the mirror above the sink. Then a naughty smile curved her luscious mouth. "Hey, handsome. You snuck up on me."

His couldn't drag his eyes from the rounded globes of her breasts revealed by her reflection. "I did." He dipped his head to run his nose up the side of her neck, taking pleasure in the way she purred and arched to give him better access. God, she was just so freaking sexy in his arms, her body as lush and curvy as a pinup model's. She filled his hands, his arms. His heart, which had been empty and lonely for so long. Sometimes it was still unbelievable to him that she was his.

Carmela spun to face him and looped her arms around his neck, rising on tiptoe with a naughty little smile on her face, her perfect breasts brushing his chest. He deserved a medal for keeping his hands off them. "You miss me?"

He was already rock-hard in his jeans, his body revved and raring to claim her, remind her she was his. "You know I did."

"Hmmm. I missed you too." She settled her lips on his, applying light pressure before sucking on his lower one for a moment.

Sawyer groaned and pulled her closer with one arm

banded around her waist, plastering her naked curves to the front of his body. When even that wasn't enough, he lifted her and turned them to pin her against the wall with his weight.

Laughing, Carmela wrapped her smooth legs around his waist and rubbed her pelvis against his steely erection. "Wow, you really did miss me."

He had. And he wasn't playing.

He made a low sound of agreement and sought her mouth again, spearing one hand in the thick mass of her hair and plunging his tongue between her full lips. He wanted inside her in the worst way. She went to his head faster than a triple shot of whiskey, and loved driving him out of his skull by teasing him until he broke.

Yeah, he was one lucky sonofabitch.

Her tongue slid along his, those gorgeous, full breasts pillowed against his chest. Sawyer dropped the arm at her waist and curved a hand around one round ass cheek, squeezing it, pulling her tighter to his erection, already dreaming of the moment when he sank into the heat he could feel through his jeans. She'd been gone for ten days and he was starving for her.

But Carm broke the kiss far too soon and gave him one of those sultry smiles that tied him in knots. The one that promised a torturous wait before the main event, when all he wanted to do was pounce. "How was the barbecue?"

He didn't care about the fucking barbecue, he just wanted to get naked and inside her as soon as possible. "What barbecue?" he murmured, only half-joking. His stomach was still full to bursting.

She laughed lightly, the erotic, seductive sound going straight to his aching cock. "My mom called before I got in the shower. She's disappointed you won't be here when she arrives."

"I'll only be gone a couple days," he muttered,

seeking her mouth again. Less talking, more sexy times. They only had until noon tomorrow before he left with his team for a training school in Nevada. Why waste a moment of it talking about stuff that wasn't important? He opened his mouth on the side of her neck, scraping his teeth over a sensitive spot. *This* was the important thing.

Carm curled her fingers over the tops of his shoulders and let out a hum of enjoyment. "By the time you come home she'll have the whole wedding nailed down."

"Fine by me." He dragged his tongue across her silken skin, fighting the urge to lower her feet to the floor, drop to his knees and bury his face between her breasts.

She pushed at his shoulder, unwound her legs from his waist and set her feet on the floor. "Sawyer. Stop a second."

The thread of annoyance in her tone broke through the haze of arousal. He tamped down his impatience, hid his disappointment and raised his head, meeting her eyes. How could she want to talk right now when his body was on fire? She was aroused too, he could tell by the flush in her cheeks and the sounds she'd been making when he was kissing her neck. "What?"

She sighed, an almost hurt expression creeping over her face. "Do you seriously not care about the wedding? I mean, you don't want to be involved with the planning? Because I don't want you to accuse me later of taking over and not giving you any say."

He shrugged. "I already told you what I think." They'd been through this several times already, most recently last night on the phone. He honestly didn't know what else to say on the subject besides what he'd already told her.

She rolled her eyes. "Eloping isn't an option. My mom would freak. She's been dreaming of my wedding day even longer than I have. It has to be in a church, and there has to be a reception after with our friends and family."

"Okay," he said with another shrug. "Whatever you guys want."

She set a finger to his lips to quiet him, a spark of annoyance in her gaze. "That's not right, Sawyer. This is your wedding too."

He wasn't going to argue about this, because it was pointless and he didn't want to fight when he was leaving in just a few hours. He'd rather spend it in bed with her. He didn't love the idea of a church wedding in front of a hundred or more people he didn't even know. But if it made her happy, then okay. "As long as I get to marry you, I don't care about the rest."

It was the truth. He just didn't see why their wedding had to be such a big deal, that's all. With his and Carm's salaries combined, they were comfortable financially. But blowing that kind of cash on a big wedding made no sense to him whatsoever. And he wouldn't know ninety-five percent of the guests in attendance anyway, as they were all people from Carm's old neighborhood back in Miami.

He understood now that a white-dress, church wedding was a big deal not only to Carm and Mama Cruz, but in the Puerto Rican culture as well, so he respected that. The two of them had compiled a freaking binder together, full of ideas and various scenarios that Sawyer honestly didn't give a shit about. Different churches and country clubs, color combinations, menu ideas, centerpieces and shit like that. None of which were important to him in the least and, in his opinion, were a damn waste of money.

If it were up to him, it would be just close family, a few of Carm's friends and his teammates in attendance. Something simple. Quick. Then they could spend the remainder of the budget on an awesome honeymoon and a down payment on a great house instead. He'd said it early on, then never brought it up again because it was clear she had other ideas.

Carm searched his eyes, as though weighing his truthfulness. Or maybe looking for something she wanted to see. "I want you to be happy with it. I want it to be the best day of your life."

"It will be, and I'll be happy as soon as I make you Mrs. Vance," he said, leaning down for another kiss and hoping she'd let it drop. He was starting to dread talking about the wedding.

Her lips curved into a slow smile beneath his. "I love you."

Yes. Victory. "Love you too. Now come here, woman." No more talking. He banded one arm beneath her bare butt and lifted her off her feet.

Carm let out a little squeal of surprise and delight and wound her legs around him again, the position pressing her open sex to his covered erection. He groaned into her mouth as her heat burned through the front of his jeans. He strode out of the steamy bathroom with her clinging to him, their tongues twined together, and carried her out into the living room. Bedroom sex was great, but today he wanted a change of venue to switch things up.

He set Carm down at the end of the tufted leather couch and yanked his shirt over his head. The sound of approval and pure female appreciation as she stared at his bare chest with naked yearning shunted every last drop of blood to his cock. He'd never get tired of the way she looked at him.

Her hands went to the fly of his jeans, impatiently ripping the button free. Sawyer plunged one hand into her hair as she shoved his jeans and underwear down his hips, kissing her with all the pent-up hunger inside him as he cupped one luscious breast in his palm and squeezed gently.

She gasped into his mouth when he tweaked the

hardened nipple, murmured when he kicked his jeans and boxers away and bent her backward over the arm of the couch, forcing her back into a gorgeous arch and elevating her breasts.

It was an invitation he couldn't resist.

He sucked one tight brown nipple into his mouth, her sexy moan mixing with the rush of blood in his ears. Christ, she was sexy. Ripe in a way he couldn't get enough of. Everything about her was sensual, but the way she responded to him, the way she never held back, turned him on more than anything. He'd felt so damn guilty about fantasizing over his best friend's sister for all that time, and now he didn't have to because she was his.

Carmela purred her approval, her fingers rubbing against his scalp as he feasted on her breasts, first one, then the other. The position gave him perfect access to her body, his hips settled between her parted thighs, his cock snug against her core. He rocked against her slowly as he suckled, sliding along her open folds.

"Ooh, Sawyer," she gasped, squirming, unable to move much with the arm of the couch beneath her and his weight pinning her in place. Being restrained did it for her in a big way, and he was happy to oblige in the fulfillment of that fantasy. He loved taking control in bed.

When her gasps and sighs turned to moans and she couldn't keep still, Sawyer gripped her hips and dropped to his knees, his face level with the tantalizing folds between her thighs. At the first touch of his lips she sucked in a sharp breath, one hand grabbing the back of his head.

With a low, possessive growl that came straight from his gut, he feasted on her, sliding his tongue over every sensitive inch of her, sucking at the taut bud peeking out before plunging his tongue inside her.

She cried out and pushed her hips up, demanding more. He kept going until she was panting, desperate, then stood. Carm reclined on the tobacco-colored leather like a centerfold, her breasts heaving with each ragged breath, eyes glazed with need, thighs splayed open over the arm of the couch.

Seeing that need on her face ignited the most primal part of him. The one that wanted to take her, claim her, brand her with his body.

Sliding his arms beneath her, he lifted her slightly and spun her over onto her stomach, her stomach resting over the arm of the couch. She wiggled her hips in blatant invitation, impatient and restless. A low sound of approval rumbled out of him as he took in the view, all that gorgeous hair spilling down her back, her forearms resting on the couch, her ass up, sex exposed to his hungry gaze.

He set his left hand on her lower back and fisted his cock, bringing it to her entrance. Carm turned her head to watch, her cheeks flushed, teeth sunk into her lower lip, her expression and the tension in her body full of breathless anticipation. Primed and ready for him. And being able to take her without any barrier between them, was so hot he couldn't control the shudder that sped through his muscles.

With one slow, firm thrust, he buried his length inside her. Soft, wet heat enveloped him in a tender caress that stole his breath and sent pleasure exploding through him. Carmela mewled and pushed backward, her eyes drifting closed, the muscles along her spine and shoulders straining.

So wet. So tight. Sawyer sucked in a breath and wrapped his hands around her hips, withdrawing almost all the way out, then pausing before surging back inside. Angling his stroke so the head of him slid over just the right spot.

"Oh, God," she moaned, coming up on her hands now to rock backward. Demanding more. Craving more of what he made her feel.

Heart thudding, he eased one hand around to cup her in his palm, settling his middle finger over her swollen clit, and pressed as he thrust forward once more.

"Saw*yerrrr*," she cried, throwing her head back, fingers digging into the leather as she moved into his thrusts, desperate for release.

Oh, hell, yeah. He loved it when she was so vocal about her pleasure, letting him know how much she enjoyed what he did to her. And he loved seeing her like this, all desperate and wild.

He growled in response and buried his face in the curve of her neck, scraping his teeth along her delicate skin, reveled in the shiver that rippled through her. She clenched around him, the increase in friction making every slick thrust hotter, until the pleasure burned like fire up his spine.

A little more pressure from his finger against her clit, every motion of their hips rubbing it along the sensitive bundle of nerves, and…yeah. Carmela pulled in a gasping breath and let out a sob as she started coming, her cries of release filling him with a soul-deep sense of satisfaction he'd never felt with anyone else.

Pulling his hand from between her thighs, he wrapped both arms around her waist, pinning her upper body to the couch as he drove deeper, faster, going after his own orgasm. Heat coiled low in his belly, spreading outward, every muscle in his body tightening in an agony of need. She was like wet silk around him, soft and sated, her hips moving lazily with his as she drifted on the currents of pleasure.

Carmela turned her head to look at him over one shoulder, her thick, dark hair tousled around her flushed face, those golden-brown eyes full of sultry promise. "I love the way your thick, hard cock feels inside me," she murmured in a desire-roughened voice.

The words zapped his nervous system like an electrical shock. He dug his fingers into her hips and drove deep, a gruff shout tearing from his throat as the pleasure swelled then burst, sending pulses of ecstasy exploding through his body.

Breathing hard, a little weak in the knees, he rested his face in the curve of her shoulder, still lodged deep inside her. She felt so good and his entire body was loose with contentment.

He couldn't wait to marry her and spend the rest of their lives loving each other like this. To be a permanent part a loving family, and maybe one day make one of their own. They'd talked about having kids, but not right away. They both wanted more time together as a couple first.

She laughed softly and wriggled beneath him. "If you're gonna fall asleep, can we switch positions so I'm not squashed over the couch?"

Sawyer barely had the strength to move. "I'm not gonna fall asleep," he mumbled.

"Yeah you are," she said with the hint of a smile in her voice.

He groaned softly. Much as he hated to pull out of her warmth, he did, and tugged her forward off the arm, helping her turn onto her side with her spine pressed to the back of the couch. Then he stretched out in front of her, tucked her head into his shoulder and tugged the blanket draped along the back of the couch on top of them. Carmela made a blissful sound and snuggled in closer, her gentle hand stroking up and down his ribs in a soothing rhythm.

This was as close to heaven as a man could get on earth. Carmela was his miracle.

She didn't speak, her hand still caressing his side. He only meant to rest his eyes for a few minutes, but it was so quiet now, just the sound of their relaxed breathing, his body was thoroughly sated and Carm's soft curves were pressed to him...

He drifted off in her arms in a matter of moments, and woke in total darkness to the shrill chime of his phone coming from the floor.

With a groan, he forced his eyes open and groped around for his jeans. What the hell time was it? Finding a denim leg, he dragged them over and fished his phone out of his pocket so he could read the message.

Hell.

"Something wrong?" Carm murmured, her fingers drifting lightly over his shoulder.

Looks like. "It's Tuck. Something's come up. They've cancelled the training and called us all into HQ right away."

Chapter Four

Nate couldn't remember ever being this content in his entire life. After years of personal turmoil, complicated by survivor's guilt and PTSD, the universe had decided to give him a break. Now it was like the stars had finally aligned for him and Taya, and everything had fallen into place.

Incredible as it seemed, every last one of his dreams had come true, professional and personal. All thanks to the woman currently about to nod off beside him in the passenger seat of his truck.

Shifting his grip on the wheel, he glanced over just in time to see Taya attempting to smother another giant yawn. The fourth over the past ten minutes. He reached for her hand, laced their fingers together. "Tired?" he said dryly. They'd stayed later than he'd anticipated, visiting with Tuck, Celida, DeLuca and Briar. Now he felt bad. Maybe he should have made their excuses and left an hour ago.

"A little."

Yeah right, a little. "You fell asleep in the middle of eating dinner. One minute I was telling the guys a story, and the next there you were, asleep with your half-full plate in your lap, fork in one hand and a drumstick in your other. And your mouth was open, too." Only a little. He couldn't resist giving her a hard time though.

She cranked her head around to stare at him, her steel gray eyes widening in alarm. "It was not."

"Totally was. I think I even saw a little trail of drool running down the side of your chin."

She playfully swatted his shoulder. "Oh, stop."

Well the first part was true. When she'd woken up a few minutes later she'd made a valiant effort at pretending she hadn't been asleep at all by continuing to eat as she fought to stay awake. The jet lag must still be hitting her, as she'd just come off another cross-country speaking tour with talks in three cities on the West Coast over the past week. Taya was in huge demand as a speaker on women's rights and her horrific experiences in Afghanistan.

Nate had never met anyone as strong as his wife, and he was damn proud of all she'd accomplished. Including how well she'd dealt with all the trauma she'd suffered. Somehow, she'd found a source of inner zen that always radiated her inner beauty and calm. Knowing how tired she was, he should have bundled her into the truck right after they'd eaten. "That trip really took it out of you, huh?"

Her smile was a little drowsy, and full of a quiet joy he could practically touch. That air of serenity she always carried with her was one of the most attractive things about her. It seemed like no matter what life threw at her, Taya just absorbed it and kept moving forward, always choosing to look at the bright side of things. "Sorry. I just couldn't keep my eyes open a second longer."

"Don't worry about it, no one minded." He squeezed her hand, still in awe of all the miracles she'd brought into his life. "You need to start getting more rest. Slow down more." He'd tried to get her to stay home today to catch up on her sleep, but she'd insisted she come to the barbecue to see everyone.

She sighed. "I know I do. It's just hard. I've got so many requests for speaking engagements I want to do."

"Well you won't be able to do any of them if you get exhausted and make yourself sick."

She aimed a tender smile at him. "I'm not fragile, Nathan."

"I know that." He knew it better than anyone, having seen her actions under fire, and while wounded. And then again, in the aftermath of that disastrous day at the courthouse when she'd gone to testify against Qureshi. And in a million other little ways since. "But I'm your husband, so I'm still allowed to worry about you." He couldn't help it. She was his world.

"I love that you worry about me. But just try to remember I'm only six years older than you. Not sixty." She raised a dark eyebrow. "I'm not on my last leg yet."

He laughed. "I never think about our age difference until you bring it up. Cradle robber."

Taya pulled her hand free and jabbed her fingers in his ribs, making him chuckle. "Watch it."

He caught her hand again, raised it to his lips for a kiss. "What was it you wanted to tell me, by the way? Before, on the way over there." She'd started to mention something on the way to DeLuca and Briar's place, but he'd received a phone call and they hadn't resumed the conversation.

She was quiet for a minute. So quiet he looked over at her in surprise. Then she cast him a sidelong glance, and her hesitation in answering made him frown. Taya never withheld anything from him. "What?" he asked.

She turned a little in her seat to look at him. "So…your sister contacted me."

The quiet admission blindsided him, bursting the warm, happy bubble he'd been floating in since Taya had arrived at the airport last night. Anger and denial punched through him, an instinctive and unstoppable reaction to the news.

He clenched his left hand around the steering wheel, suspicion coiling in the pit of his stomach. "When?" he demanded, jaw tight. Maybe he'd heard wrong.

Her expression turned worried. "Yesterday morning, just before checkout. She emailed me."

She'd looked up Taya's email address? "What? How the hell did she even find out about you?" They'd only been married a couple months, and he sure as shit hadn't told Dara.

"She said she saw an interview of mine on TV and looked me up. She contacted me through my website."

His jaw flexed. He didn't like the feel of this. "What did she want?" There had to be an angle. With his sister, there always was, and always would be. Three years older than him, she'd been raised from the cradle to be a master liar, manipulator and user. A carefully trained carbon copy of their mother.

"Nathan," Taya chided at his harsh tone.

"No." He didn't care if he sounded like an asshole. Taya didn't get it. Always the peacemaker, wanting to smooth everything over, fix it all. Well, some things couldn't be fixed. Or forgiven. And never forgotten. He pulled in a steadying breath and fought to hold onto his patience. "What did she *want*?"

"She wanted to verify that I really was your wife, and then she asked about you."

"What about me?"

She shrugged. "Just general things. How you were doing, where we were living."

He shot her a look, rattled at the news. "Tell me you didn't answer that last one."

"I just said we were in the D.C. area. Okay, I shouldn't have told her even that much, but I didn't think it was that big a deal since it's vague, and she knows you must be close to here anyway because of your job."

Nate sucked in a deep breath through his nose and tried to calm down, but it was no use. The last time he'd heard from Dara was when their mother had died last year. Because she'd had no way to contact him she'd reached out to the FBI to pass along the message that she was looking for him.

He hadn't answered. Hadn't even attended the funeral, no matter how much Taya had tried to reason with him, saying it would bring him a sense of peace and closure. Always trying to see the best in people and give them a second chance. But why would he go, when the woman who'd given birth to him had been dead to him for years now?

"She wants money," he said flatly. That was usually Dara's prime motivation.

"You don't know that."

"I *do* know that." And it pissed him off that Taya would question his judgment on this. She didn't know Dara, hadn't grown up with her. He'd purposely cut his mother and sister out of his life a long time ago, back when he'd left and joined the Air Force, and it was the best thing he'd ever done, other than marrying Taya.

A week after the funeral, Dara's lawyer had sent him paperwork about his half of the inheritance, less than two thousand bucks that Nate hadn't collected. Dara wanted it, and she wouldn't stop until she got what she wanted. And even then she'd keep going, keep searching, see what else she could get from Nate or anyone else she might be able to collect from. It made him sick.

At his angry tone Taya went quiet and turned away to look out her window. Nate reined in his temper with effort. He wasn't mad at Taya. But the news had taken him off guard and hit a raw spot inside him. It infuriated him that his sister would stoop to try and weasel her way back into his life now through Taya, who didn't realize she was being taken advantage of. Dara smelled that kind of opening a mile away and seized on it like the predator she was.

"If she contacts you again, ignore her." It was important Taya understand how toxic his sister was. "Dara is selfish and a user, on top of being an expert manipulator." She'd learned it all from the best, after all. No one played people or the system like Janet Schroder had. "I don't want her in my life, period, and especially not now. I don't want her to touch us. Ever."

"I was just being polite. It's not like I asked her to come up and visit us."

He didn't care. "Swear you won't talk to her again."

Taya gazed at him a long moment, studying him, then relented with a nod. "All right," she said, her voice soft. "I promise. And I'm sorry. I didn't mean to stir up trouble."

He knew that. But her promise to avoid contact with Dara only mollified him a little. He was still stewing about his useless and calculating relative when they got home. Taya met him around the front of the truck, her gray eyes searching his.

If she was waiting for an apology for his reaction or stance on the issue, she was in for a disappointment. The shit he'd gone through with his family for all those years ran too deep and he wasn't going to change his mind about this, not even for his wife.

But instead of pressing him for answers, Taya slipped her arms around his neck and hugged him, pressing her sweet body into his. And just like that, Nate calmed, a long exhalation rushing from him as he wrapped his arms around her. After a few moments, the worst of the anger drained away. He held her to him, breathing in her cinnamon-vanilla scent, drinking in that uncanny sense of peace she always had about her.

This was honest and real. The past couldn't touch them anymore, unless he allowed it to.

"I hit a nerve there, huh?" she murmured against his shoulder.

"Yeah." A big one.

He wasn't proud of it. Most of his issues he'd dealt with. But some were too ingrained and he didn't feel like wasting energy on them.

He searched for the right words. "It's just…you don't know how toxic things were when I was growing up." The constant shame when landlords had come to evict them from yet another place, knowing his mother had used up all her lies and they had to move on again. Or when the creditors had come after them and repossessed their stuff.

His mother had been a pro at working the welfare system, but even her maneuvering had its limits. He'd told Taya about most of it, but hearing about it wasn't the same as living it. He'd sworn to himself that the moment he was old enough, he'd leave and never look back. And he hadn't.

The words kept coming. "I did everything in my power to escape all that, and I'm not going to let anything jeopardize what we have now."

She nodded, easing back to meet and hold his gaze. "I understand."

No, she didn't, not really. How could she, when she'd grown up in a loving, supportive home, and was still close to her father and brother? And he didn't want her to. But he appreciated that she was trying to see where he was coming from. That she had his back. It calmed him.

He ran a hand through her long brown curls, the strands wrapping around his fingers. Clinging, as if they didn't want to let go. He knew the feeling. "You're wiped.

Let's get you to bed."

"Okay, Doc."

"Hey." He swatted her butt gently, loving the way her eyes sparkled with humor. "Only the guys get to call me that. Not you." With a grin, he dropped a light kiss on her lips and tugged her toward the door.

The mention of his past had stirred up a lot of memories best left buried. He resented that even more considering he was leaving tomorrow for a training op, and had only a few hours left to spend with Taya.

To clear his head, he hopped in the shower, stood there letting the hot water beat down on him. The past was the past. He and Taya had a bright future to look forward to. *They* were what mattered. Thinking about his sister for one second longer was pointless.

Toweling off his hair, he walked back into the master bedroom and stopped in the doorway, his heart turning over when he saw his wife. Taya was stretched out on her side on top of the covers still wearing all her clothes, and fast asleep. She looked like an angel lying there, her hair spilling over the pillow, the thin, silvery scars on the side of her face revealed in the soft light from the bedside lamp.

He rarely noticed her scars anymore, but not a day went by when he didn't think about how she'd gotten them, and he'd always wonder why he'd come through their ordeal in Afghanistan unscathed when she'd suffered so much and he's lost the man who'd been like his brother.

Well, physically Nate had been unscathed, anyway. He still had some residual survivor's guilt about O'Neil, but Taya had helped with a lot of it, and he still journaled whenever the issue reared its head again.

God, he owed her everything. Could never in ten lifetimes give her back as much as she'd given him. But he'd sure as hell try.

As gently as he could, he turned her onto her back, smiling down into her face when she stirred and blinked up at him with dazed, gray eyes. "You're still dressed," he whispered, hoping to not wake her up completely as he removed her socks. He'd planned to make love to her, had been thinking about it all afternoon, but if she was this tired he would let her sleep.

Taya gave a drowsy sigh, didn't respond as she allowed him to help her undress and get her under the covers. He thought she was asleep again when he crawled in beside her naked and pulled her to his chest, then switched off the bedside lamp, a faint amount of light filtering in through the open door from the bathroom window.

"Nathan?"

He stilled. "Yeah?"

"I have something else to tell you."

He tensed, suddenly wary, his mind automatically bracing for more about Dara. He didn't want to hear it, but he also needed to let Taya say her piece. "Okay."

"I hope it's better news than the last bit."

Me too. He ran a hand over her hair. "So? What is it?"

She shifted until she was lying on her side facing him, her head on his pillow, her gaze on his. "I'm pregnant."

Nate stopped breathing. He stared at his wife's face in the faint light, his mind wiped blank. "What?"

Gentle fingers trailed over his cheek, down to stroke his lips, and there was a smile in her voice as she answered. "We're going to have a baby."

Joy burst inside him. "Oh, my God, Taya…" He locked his arms around her and dragged her to him, cradling her as close as he could. Was this real? He wasn't dreaming? "You're sure?"

Her curls brushed the bottom of his chin as she

nodded. "Positive. I took two tests yesterday morning before checking out of my hotel. I think I'm around five weeks or so."

Unexpected tears burned his eyes. "Oh, my God," he repeated with a little laugh. He was going to be a father? It had happened so fast.

She snuggled into him. "So you're happy?"

She had to ask? "God, yes. I'm freaking thrilled. What about you?"

"I'm *so* excited," she gushed, the tremor of excitement in her voice contagious. "I was dying to tell you, but I thought I'd better tell you the other thing first, and then it just didn't seem like the right time…"

Because he'd been so angry she'd worried that he wouldn't have given her this reaction. Guilt hit him. She'd been waiting to tell him since yesterday morning, and he'd spoiled the big moment for her with his reaction to the news about Dara.

He buried his face in her hair. "I'm sorry I was a dick when you told me about her. But this is even more reason to cut my sister out of our lives once and for all."

Taya kissed his neck, sending an instant rush of heat to his groin. He loved the feel of her mouth on him, even the G-rated parts. Of course, he loved the feel of it on his X-rated parts *more*. "It's okay, I get it."

He did his best to ignore the blast of arousal she'd triggered, and focus on the happy news. *Pregnant.* Damn, had he been too rough with her last night? He'd been so worked up after being apart for two weeks, and she'd seemed just as hungry for him. Gliding his hand down her ribs, he splayed his palm protectively over the slight curve of her abdomen.

Their baby. Tucked safely inside her. It was too incredible. "Are you feeling okay? You're not sick or anything?"

"Not really, only a little if I get too hungry. Mostly

just tired. And my boobs are a little sore."

No wonder she was so exhausted. "When's the due date, do you know?" Man, under a year from now they were going to be parents. Unreal.

"Mid-summer, I think. Probably in the first half of July. I'm going to see my doctor on Monday, so I'll know more then."

"I'll go with you."

"You'll be out of town."

Ah, hell. "Then call me from the office as soon as you find out."

"I will."

He drew her back into his arms, overwhelmed with love and gratitude. "God, I love you so much."

"I love you so much too." The words ended with another huge yawn.

Chuckling, Nate kissed the top of her head. "Go to sleep, baby." He held her close while she melted into his body and drifted off in his arms.

Savoring the peace washing over him, he nuzzled her curls and lay there staring into the darkness, enjoying the feel of his wife's warm, curvy body snuggled into him. His incredible little warrior. The mother of his child.

He didn't remember falling asleep. One minute he was holding Taya, the next his head jerked up from the pillow when his phone went off from the bathroom. He jumped up and hurried to check it, saw the message there from Tuck.

911. Training op canceled. Report to base at 04:00.

Nate rubbed a hand over his eyes, fighting a groan. It was already 02:50 now. Just enough time to get dressed, grab his gear and get to base. What was going on? Something pretty big must have come up to call them in now and cancel the training op. He'd listen to the news on his way in.

Taya stirred when he sat beside her on the bed,

blinked up at him sleepily in the light coming from the open bathroom door. "What's wrong?" she murmured, coming up on one elbow, squinting in the faint light.

"Training's been canceled. We've been called in to HQ for something. Not sure what."

Her eyes cleared and she sat up, but he stopped her, pressing her shoulders back down onto the mattress. "No, you stay here and get some more sleep."

"You sure? I can help you pack."

"I'm sure." He leaned over her, kissed her forehead and the bridge of her nose before finally capturing her lips with his.

She softened, her mouth warm and inviting as she curled a hand around the back of his neck. God, he loved this woman. She was without a doubt the kindest, most courageous person he'd ever known. No way he deserved her, but he hoped he never gave her reason to figure that out.

"I'll call you with details when I can," he whispered. "Not sure when I'll be back, but it could be a few days if they're sending us out."

"Okay. Love you."

"Love you too." He slid a hand into her curls, hating to go so soon. "You'll be okay?" A ridiculous question, but he couldn't help asking.

She shook her head at him slightly, amusement brimming in her eyes. "Really?"

He grinned. "Yeah, that was stupid. Pretend I never said it."

Cupping her chin in his hand, he kissed her once more, then pulled the covers aside, somehow mustered up the willpower to merely graze his lips over the curves of her breasts and pass by her hardening nipples on his way to her abdomen. He nuzzled her velvety soft skin there, pressed a kiss to the spot just below her belly button where their child slept, and tucked her back in to avoid the sweet temptation her naked body presented. "See you soon."

She nodded. "Be safe."

"I will."

He went to the closet to put on his tactical uniform and grab his gear. When he looked back from the bathroom a few minutes later, where he'd paused to shut the light off, Taya was fast asleep again. Nate smiled, drinking in the sight of her for one moment longer before hitting the switch. In the darkness, he hesitated, the image of her curled up in their bed burned into his mind.

He always hated leaving her, but this time the urge to stay was so strong he had to force himself to walk away and out the door.

Chapter Five

Agent Brad Tucker was in the master bedroom closet packing the last of his gear when the call came in. The text prior to it had woken him from a dead sleep five minutes ago in his bed. His empty bed. Even at two in the morning the other side of it was still undisturbed, the covers all neatly in place, telling him Celida hadn't come to bed yet. Burning the midnight oil and then some on the case she was currently working on.

Tuck checked his phone. No surprise, his commander's number showed on the screen. Never a good sign when DeLuca called at this time of night. "Tuck here," he answered, grabbing a second tactical shirt from the shelf.

"Got an update," DeLuca said over the rumble of voices in the background. "You and the boys will be heading to Atlanta as soon as we can get you on a flight down there. I'm about to hop a transport. I'll meet you all at the head office there with more detailed intel."

"Sounds good." He walked to the bathroom, his mind

clear but his body protesting being hauled out of bed during a night he was supposed to be able to sleep in. Nights at home were precious, and he savored them all. Just sucked that he hadn't spent it tangled up in bed with his wife. "Any details I can pass to the guys?" Although he had a pretty good idea what this was about.

"You heard about the hostage situation with a barricaded subject in a rural area outside Atlanta?"

"Yeah." It had been on the news last night, he and Celida had heard about it on the way home from the team barbecue. A Bureau SWAT team had been deployed along with the rest of the usual taskforce for that kind of situation. Things must have escalated substantially overnight if Tuck's team was being called in. The HRT was the U.S.'s premier civilian unit for responding to hostage crises and other high-risk situations. They only got deployed when the stakes were high.

"Well, things started to go to hell a couple hours ago. Just got confirmation that negotiations have failed. Suspect has cut off contact with agents and is threatening to kill anyone who approaches the cabin. He's former MARSOC and heavily armed, so we got the call."

"I'll let the guys know. Call you once I get to base."

After getting ready and grabbing his gear, he headed out of the bedroom. He found Celida at the kitchen table, her cheek propped in one hand as she stared at her glowing laptop screen. She glanced over at him when he entered, her eyes bleary.

"Still up?"

She gave a tired smile and rubbed at the back of her neck. "Unfortunately. That DeLuca?"

Tuck nodded and closed the distance between them. He pushed her hand away and took over massaging the back of her neck, earning a grateful groan that ended in a sensual purr. Damn shame he didn't have time to pick her up, carry her back into their room and make her feel even better. "Team's being deployed to Atlanta."

Her shoulders stiffened. "Is it the barricaded Marine?"

"Yeah."

She blew out a breath. "Thought so. DeLuca say what's going on?"

"Just that the suspect cut all contact with negotiators."

"Yeah, I would too if an FBI sniper shot my daughter."

Tuck's insides went cold, his hands stilling on her shoulders. "What?"

Celida turned her laptop screen toward him. He stepped to the side and gripped the edge of the circular table as he bent forward to read the message from one of her FBI contacts. "Son of a bitch," he muttered. One of their SWAT snipers had shot the suspect's teenage daughter by mistake when she'd stepped out onto the back porch. "How bad is she?" he asked, scanning the rest of the email. Information was sketchy.

"According to my source it was a center mass shot, so she's probably critical. The father is providing medical assistance, but won't let anyone approach the residence to help."

Any trust the man might have had in the federal officers and first responders had been destroyed with the bullet that had struck his daughter, and like Celida, Tuck couldn't say he blamed him. *Hell...*

He cursed and straightened, dragging a hand over his face. It was shades of Ruby Ridge all over again, a nightmare and public relations disaster the Bureau was still trying to recover from. The media and public would go apeshit if the report was true. "DeLuca didn't mention anything about this."

"He probably doesn't know yet. But I'll bet he'll be getting the call any minute now."

Tuck set his hands on his hips. *Dammit*. This put his team in more danger in an already volatile and high-risk situation. "How many other people are in the cabin?"

"Including the suspect, last count was four—him, the wife, and two younger kids. Twins." She twisted her head to look up at him, concern in her bloodshot, deep gray eyes. "I'll keep monitoring it on my end. If I hear anything else important I'll text you."

Be careful, Tuck.

She didn't say it, but the words were clear in her expression and it warmed him inside. As a fellow special agent and his former partner, Celida understood him better than any other woman could have. She knew exactly the kinds of danger his job entailed, and though she handled it well, she still worried.

It just made him love her that much more.

"You should go to bed," he murmured, brushing a lock of coffee-brown hair back from her right cheek to expose the long-healed bullet graze there. She had shadows under her eyes, the result of too many all-nighters recently.

She shook her head, the stubborn tilt of her chin both familiar and endearing. "Not when you're heading down there to deal with this."

There was no point arguing with her about it. With Celida he had to pick his battles, and he already knew this was one he wouldn't win. She would sit here at her computer with her cell next to her, watching for any intel that might be useful to him. And she wouldn't sleep until he called to tell her the job was done, and that he was safe. Just another thing in the long list of why he adored her.

He took her face in his hands. "I ever tell you I love you?"

"No."

His lips quirked at her serious tone. Always so saucy. She never complained about his job, the insane hours it demanded, or how often they were apart. It meant a lot that she fully supported him in his career, just as he supported hers. "Well I do."

She curled her fingers around his wrists and leaned her cheek into his right palm. "Love you back." She released one of his wrists to cup the back of his head and pull him into a hard kiss, then let go and eased away. "You watch yourselves out there."

"Will do." His team's safety was paramount, and the most important part of his role as team leader. Taking care of his guys and making sure they all went home safe at the end of the day was always his top priority. The mission came second. "Bye. I'll call you when we get to Atlanta, give you an update. Probably be gone for at least a couple days."

"Just come home safe."

"You know it, sunshine. Miss me." He dropped another kiss on her upturned lips then grabbed his gear and walked out into the cool pre-dawn darkness to face yet another mission and its uncertain outcome.

****

Distant honking made Nate look up just as a V-formation of geese flew overhead in the pre-dawn sky, heading south for warmer climates now that fall was here.

Still overwhelmed by the news of becoming a father, he hoisted the straps of his bags higher onto his right shoulder and followed his teammates across the darkened tarmac toward the waiting Air Force C-130 parked near the end of the runway. DeLuca had briefed them via speakerphone from Atlanta, and arranged this flight for them. Between then and now, things down there had gotten damn ugly.

Rumors had been flying around that a SWAT sniper had shot the suspect's teenage daughter when she'd stepped out onto the porch wearing her father's hat and hunting jacket. Five minutes before leaving base, DeLuca had called back to say the fourteen-year-old had subsequently died.

Now the grieving father was even more traumatized and unpredictable. He'd threatened to blow up the side of the mountain his home sat on rather than surrender, and refused to allow his wife and two remaining children to leave, or to allow anyone to take away his daughter's body. Right now, the teenage girl was wrapped in a plastic tarp, lying in the middle of the living room.

That was the scene Nate's team would confront in a few more hours, and he'd be lying if he said he didn't have a gut-deep, bad feeling about this one. Dog teams and explosive ordinance disposal units were on site to search and clear the area below the cabin, but they could only do so much, and if they got too close, the suspect would likely open fire on them. So if Nate and his teammates received the order to make the assault and moved in, they'd be going in blind.

The C-130's tail ramp was down, other members of the critical incident response group already on board. Nate strode up it, stored his gear, then planted his ass in a jump seat along the left-hand wall beside Bauer. Maybe not such a great idea, since Bauer was freaking huge, his shoulder shoved up against Nate's. Too late to move now, though, because Tuck sat on Nate's other side, taking the last empty seat.

Bauer was too bulky and hard to make for a comfy pillow. Covering a yawn, Nate folded his hands atop his belly, leaned his head back and closed his eyes, intending to catch some Zs on the way to Atlanta. But as the ramp closed and the engines throttled up, sending vibrations through the deck of the aircraft, he thought about Taya and found himself smiling secretly.

Bauer elbowed the side of Nate's arm. "What's

funny?"

"Nothing," he said without opening his eyes. "Just happy."

"Yeah?" Tuck said from his left. "What about?"

Nate opened his eyes and turned his head toward his team leader, his smile widening. "Taya's pregnant."

Tuck's eyes widened, his dark blond eyebrows shooting upward. "Are you serious?"

"Yep. Five weeks."

As Tuck grinned, Bauer slapped a big hand on Nate's shoulder, gave him a little shake that would have rattled a lesser man's teeth. "That's so awesome, man. Happy for you guys."

"Thanks." He couldn't wipe the grin from his face. He was gonna be a father in a few months' time.

"Happy for who? And for what?" Cruzie called out from across the cargo hold, seated between Vance and Evers, who were all staring at Nate with curiosity.

"Nate and Taya. Doc's gonna be a daddy," Tuck announced to the entire cargo bay.

Twenty-three pairs of eyes turned toward him, five of them familiar, the others not. A chorus of whistles and congrats filled the cavernous space and he lifted a hand in acknowledgment.

"Were you guys trying?" Blackwell asked from Bauer's right, leaning forward and craning his neck to see Nate past Bauer's bulk.

"Not officially. We both wanted to start a family soon, so we decided to pull the goalie a few months ago. Never thought it would happen so quick." The news had come as a shock. He'd assumed it would take a while. They'd only been married a few months, tying the knot in a small wedding on her dad's farm back in Kentucky, with only DeLuca and Briar there for Nate. He hadn't wanted to drag the entire team down there just for them, but he appreciated his commander and wife being there.

"When did you find out?" Evers asked.

"Few hours ago." Nate still couldn't believe she'd managed to wait that long. She'd been so damn excited about it.

"It's life changing, man," Bauer said in his deep voice, folding his thick arms across his chest and giving Nate a couple inches more elbow room. "It's gonna be so awesome, you'll love it."

"Except for the no-sleep part, right?" Bauer bitched about that all the time, and the guys constantly gave him a hard time about it. It was how they showed the love.

Bauer's hard mouth twisted into a wry grin. "Yeah, except that. But hey, sleep deprivation's nothing new for guys like us."

No, it wasn't. He'd be fine.

"You're gonna be a great daddy," Tuck said with a slap to Nate's leg.

"Thanks." He'd do his best. He didn't remember his father, but Taya's dad was awesome, and both Bauer and Blackwell were pretty damn good examples to follow. DeLuca, too, because Nate pretty much idolized him. He'd figure it out, basically do the opposite of what his mother had. That would be a good start, anyhow.

"The whole birthing thing is no joke though, man," Bauer added. "With your medical background you'll be fine. That stuff's way more up your alley than mine." He winced, shook his dark head. "Zo's already talking about baby number two, but for damn sure I'm not ready to go through all that again."

"*You're* not ready to go through it again?" Nate said with a laugh.

"Dude." Bauer half-turned toward him, his bright blue eyes serious. "You ever witness a birth?"

"A few, yeah." Once at a hospital during one of his training rotations, and a couple times during his service as a PJ.

Bauer blinked at him in surprise, then sobered. "Well have you ever seen one when it's your wife and kid involved?"

Okay, he had a point there. "No."

"Yeah, well. Wait for it. It ain't pretty." He shook his head again, that hard mouth twisting in distaste. "I've seen things, man. Things you can't unsee."

It tickled Nate's funny bone, to think of a badass former SEAL like Bauer going pale and weak in the knees at witnessing the birth of his own child after all the violent, gory and fucked-up things he'd seen over the course of his career. Bauer was no stranger to blood and guts. None of them were.

"That's funny?" Bauer said, raising a dark eyebrow when Nate smirked.

"So freaking funny," Nate said with a chuckle that turned into a full-on belly laugh the more he pictured his teammate's reaction in the delivery room.

The laugh must have been infectious because all his teammates started grinning and chuckling too. Nate couldn't help himself. Couldn't stop now that he'd got going.

"Poor Zoe," he managed between gasps, holding his aching middle as he imagined the scene in the delivery room. "She's the one in agony, trying to hold it together while she pushes Libby out, and her former SEAL husband can't handle it."

Bauer's brows snapped together in a foreboding frown that didn't intimidate Nate in the least. "I handled it. I handled it fine—*better* than fine. She told me I was awesome."

That only made Nate hoot louder. Zoe having to soothe Bauer's giant ego afterward by praising his efforts at trying not to be a useless boob during the delivery. He wiped his watering eyes with the heel of one hand. "Did you at least find your balls long enough to cut the cord?"

Bauer's jaw clenched and he turned his head away, facing the others across the cargo hold. "I didn't have the option."

Huh? "Why not?" Had there been some kind of complication Nate hadn't heard about, and the docs had taken over?

Big guy still wouldn't look at him, seemed to flounder for the right words. Not that Bauer was very wordy in the first place. "I was...busy doing other shit, okay?"

"Yeah? Like what?" Because Nate couldn't imagine not doing that honor. He planned to be right in there during the birth, couldn't wait to help bring their child into the world. His biggest problem was going to be resisting the urge to take over from the doc and nurses.

Bauer waved a hand around in exasperation. "Shit was going down, all right? Zoe was screaming, and there was blood everywhere—and yeah, it's way different when it's your wife screaming, and it's her damn blood all over the place. Plus I was holding one of her legs back for her," he finished.

Nate still didn't understand. "After the baby came out?" That made no sense whatsoever.

Bauer's jaw worked. "Yeah, after."

"But why?" As far as he knew, women didn't need anyone to hold their legs back while delivering the placenta. That was supposedly the easy part. Or so he'd heard, and the few births he'd attended had seemed to confirm it.

Bauer was quiet a moment, his nostrils flaring. "Because I was still in my chair." he muttered in a low voice.

Wait, what? Nate stared at him, not sure he'd heard right. "They put you in a chair? What for?" Nate eyed him. *Unless...* His eyes widened as he stared at Bauer's hard face. No way. "Did you pass out?"

"What?" Cruzie called out across from them, staring avidly at Bauer. "You *fainted*?"

Answering snickers and chuckles from the rest of the team were drowned out by the plane's engines powering up.

"No," Bauer snapped, giving them all the evil eye as they began moving down the runway. "I just had to sit down for a while near the end. And fuck you all, until you've seen that happen to your wife and her lady bits, you don't know shit about it, so you can't judge." He raised his chin in defiance, bumped Blackwell with an elbow. "Blackwell gets it."

Blackwell, ever the peacemaker, slung an arm around Bauer's shoulders in silent support. He and his wife Summer had been to hell and back trying to have a baby. The entire team had been ecstatic when little Sam was born healthy without any complications. "It's okay, man, I hear you. It's intense."

"Yeah, see? It's *intense*," Bauer echoed to everyone else, arms folded across his wide chest, jaw set in defiance.

Blackwell paused a heartbeat before adding, "But I still managed to man up, stay vertical and cut the cord."

A roar of laughter rang out at the diss. The tops of Bauer's cheeks turned red, and he threw Blackwell's arm off him as the plane picked up more speed, hurtling them along the runway. "Don't touch me," he growled.

Blackwell shrugged good-naturedly and grinned. "Just giving you a hard time, brother."

"Whatever. Backstabber."

The plane's nose angled upward, easing them up into the air. Nate was still smirking to himself as he leaned his head back and closed his eyes, ready for a snooze.

He let the motion of the aircraft lull him as they climbed skyward, the lift pushing him down into the seat.

A series of loud, rapid bangs pummeled the fuselage

of the aircraft, loud as gunshots.

Nate's eyes flew open. Everyone was frozen and quiet in their seats, looking at each other.

The sound of the engines changed, dropping audibly. And then the aircraft pitched downward with enough force to practically lift them out of their seats.

Nate threw both hands down to clutch the bottom of his. He grunted when the plane suddenly jerked upward, slamming his ass down with enough force to make his teeth clack together. He reached for the nylon straps of the seatbelt to tighten it, but it was too late.

A deafening bang split the air.

The aircraft seemed to stall in midair, then tipped sharply to the left and began dropping like a stone out of the sky.

Chapter Six

"Holy shit," Nate blurted under his breath, scrambling to tighten his lap belt. There were no windows back here. He couldn't tell where they were, how far up they were. Or whether the pilots had managed to wrestle the plane around to get back to the runway in time.

All of a sudden the loadmaster appeared at the front of the cargo bay, his face grim. "Brace, brace!" he yelled, strapping himself into his own seat.

For a second Nate stared at him in disbelief. Jesus Christ, they were gonna crash?

His heart pummeled the inside of his ribs as he doubled over, put his head between his knees and clamped his hands behind the back of his neck. There was no time to panic, or pray.

He thought of Taya and their unborn child. His mind latched onto an image of her smiling up at him on their wedding day. The sun glinted off the tangle of dark curls pinned up on the crown of her head, the spray of flowers tucked there glowing in the late afternoon light. Her gray eyes were luminous as she gazed up at him, and so full of love and trust that for a moment it was hard to breathe.

His stomach lurched as the plane suddenly tipped sideways, dropping faster.

Please God, I don't want to die.

They hit the ground hard with a bone-jolting, sickening metallic crunch.

Nate's chin slammed into his right knee. Blood filled his mouth. The plane bounced upward for a second, enough time for a spurt of hope to burn through the shock.

Please, please...

But it was smothered when they smashed into the ground again a heartbeat later. His breath hitched as the aircraft flipped to the left and continued to skid on its side, the terrible scream of tearing metal shrieking in his ears as the wing behind him was ground away.

The lights went out, dropping them into complete blackness that was even more disorienting when the aircraft flipped upside down and kept sliding.

Nate squeezed his eyes shut and hung on, now upside down in the jump seat and held in only by the belt across his lap. He swallowed more blood, his heart lodged at the top of his throat. It seemed to go on forever, the broken fuselage bouncing and pitching along the ground. Finally it lurched to a stop, wrenching another grunt out of him as it snapped him sideways in his seat toward the cockpit.

In the eerie, stygian blackness, it took a moment to register that they'd stopped. That he was still alive.

He thrust one hand up to brace himself against the ceiling, and fumbled with the other to get the buckle of the lap belt undone.

"Anyone hurt?" Tuck called out beside him.

Groans and cries of pain answered him, then a few positive responses.

Nate winced as his head and shoulder slammed into

the roof when the buckle released. He scrambled to his feet, shot a hand out to grab for something to orient himself with. It landed on something hard and solid. A shoulder.

He squeezed tight. "Bauer?"

"Yeah. I'm...okay." His teammate was struggling to find his footing.

"Doc, you good?" Tuck asked from his left.

"Yep." Who was hurt? He glanced toward the closed tail ramp. No way they were getting out that way. Searching around, his gaze caught on a small amount of daylight coming in across from him. A hole had been torn into the belly of the starboard side fuselage, just behind the wing.

The groans and cries around him grew louder, mixed with frantic, stressed voices from the other taskforce members onboard. Nate started toward the opening, barely able to tell which way was up. But they had to get out in case—

The unmistakable scent of smoke and jet fuel hit him.

His chest constricted. *Fuck.* "Everybody get out, right now." He lurched forward, struggling to find his footing in this strange new terrain. "There's a fire."

Someone was already at the opening, banging at the side of the aircraft. Coming closer, Nate made out the silhouette of someone struggling to get the emergency exit door open. "It's jammed," the familiar voice said. Cruzie.

Nate headed over to help, bumped into someone on the way. He didn't stop to see who it was, just made for the door as fast as he could. All the gear they'd brought on board was scattered all over the place, rendering any of their tools and equipment useless because they couldn't spare the time in searching for any of it.

Together, he, Cruzie and the third man shoved and fought with the hatch. Nate gritted his teeth, his back, arms and legs straining against the unforgiving wall of metal standing between them and freedom.

A small explosion sounded up near the cockpit, sending a bolt of adrenaline surging through his veins.

Goddamn it, *no*. He was not dying in here. He wasn't burning to death, trapped in this metal coffin.

A snarl of animal determination grated in his throat as he pushed, pushed with the others.

Metal squealed as they forced the hatch outward, fraction of an inch by torturous fraction of an inch. "Again," the third man ordered.

Evers.

Nate obeyed, putting everything he had into it, knowing his life and everyone else's depended on them getting this bitch open.

Pre-dawn light streamed in through the tiny gap between the edge of the hatch and the fuselage. "Come on, you fucker," Nate growled, his entire body burning with the effort, sweat slicking his face and spine.

One more coordinated, mammoth heave and something snapped. The hatch swung open. Only a couple feet, but it was enough.

He glanced left, horror washing over him as he took in the situation outside. The plane had plowed through some trees into some sort of field, and the devastation to the front of the aircraft was hard to take in. The nose and cockpit were gone, sheared away by the force of the crash. Flames already licked at the front of the wreckage, creeping aft. Smoke billowed out in thick, black clouds that stung his eyes and the back of his throat.

Throwing an arm over his nose and mouth, Nate coughed and ducked back inside. "This way," he called out to everyone. "Go out here and run right. Get as far away from the plane as you can. *Hurry*."

His first impulse was to locate all his teammates, make sure none of them were hurt, but every moment they stayed in here increased the chances of them dying. Two of the guys had located their rifles and had switched on the tac lights, providing some illumination in the interior.

Stepping out of the way to let the others by, Nate reached for the first person who got close to him—a female. "It's about a five-foot drop," he warned her, helping her into the doorway, and wrapped a steadying arm around her waist. She was shaking, hitching in little breaths as she stared out the partially-open hatch at the ground below. "You'll have to jump." And she had to do it fast, to clear the way for the others. They didn't have much time before the flames reached the spilled fuel. A few minutes at most. Maybe less.

She nodded, gripped the sides of the opening, and when he let go, jumped. She hit the ground and fell to her knees, but got up and staggered away to the right, toward the edge of the field they were in. Nate reached back for the next person.

One after the other he helped the passengers escape the wreckage. Thick, acrid smoke spilled in through the open door, and it was getting damn hot out there. Too hot. Then a familiar voice called out from behind him.

"Doc, need a hand here."

Nate spun around to find Vance half-carrying an injured male agent toward the door. His teammate's face was drawn tight with pain, and the man he carried had a head wound that had covered his face with blood.

"I gotcha," Nate managed with a cough, grabbing hold of the injured man's waist and relieving Vance of the full burden of his weight. His other teammates were busy gathering the rest of the passengers and herding them toward the door. Nate studied Vance's face. His teammate was definitely hurt. How bad, Nate couldn't tell yet.

Come on, come on. Hurry.

They both stepped aside to let Tuck escort another female agent out of the plane. When their team leader hopped down with her, released her and turned back to them, Nate and Vance lowered their patient to him. The man's knees buckled. Without a word Tuck slung the guy over his shoulders and started hustling away from the plane.

Nate glanced left, fear starting to override his control. The flames were spreading ever closer. Even if the whole plane didn't blow, in another minute it would be impossible to escape the fire.

"We're clear. Let's haul ass, boys," Cruzie said from somewhere behind them. The remaining members of the team jumped out through the ruined hatch. Nate went last, holding his breath, squinting through the stinging smoke. The fire was spreading faster now. Thing was gonna blow any moment.

He ran after the others, heading through the battered cornfield.

Thirty yards away from the plane, he heard it. A thin, panicked cry for help behind him.

"Don't leave me! Please, *help* me!" The terror and desperation in that voice raised the hair on the back of Nate's neck.

He whipped around, scanning through the rolling smoke, shock jolting through him when his gaze landed on someone dragging himself away on his belly from the burning wreckage. The man wore a flight suit.

One of the flight crew, and he appeared to be hurt bad.

Nate started running toward him, the taste of blood strong in his mouth. Vance had stopped too, was heading back with him. Nate waved him away without slowing. He was closer than his teammate, and Vance was hurt. "I got him! You go!" Several other teammates had stopped as well, were turning back to help.

Ignoring them, Nate put his head down and ran as fast as he could, covering the distance to the man in a matter of seconds. Heat seared his face, neck and hands as he approached, but he kept going.

The wounded airman was sobbing on the ground, his legs stretched out behind him as he clawed his way toward Nate using just his arms. Poor bastard's legs were on fire.

Heat blasted Nate's skin, blistering in its intensity. He couldn't stop. He was the wounded man's only chance.

Skidding to his knees beside the man, Nate smothered the flames licking at the charred remains of his flight suit legs. There was no time to assess how bad the damage was, or worry about hurting the patient more by moving him. He reached under the man's armpits, intending to haul him up and throw him across his shoulders.

"Julian," the man cried out, twisting his head to look to the left.

Nate followed his frantic gaze, stifled a curse when he saw another crewman lying crumpled in the grass several yards away, his body partially obscured by the smoke. He was probably dead. Nate's priority was getting his patient to safety.

"I got him," a deep voice rumbled over his left shoulder.

Bauer appeared out of nowhere, grabbed hold of Nate's patient and tossed him over one broad shoulder. Ignoring the man's screams, Bauer reached down, grasped Nate's hand and yanked him to his feet before turning and running away.

Nate couldn't leave the other crewmember. The smoke was so thick he couldn't see. Holding his breath, he was forced to get on his hands and knees and blindly grope around for him. His left hand made contact with something. A leg. He gripped it, pulled, his lungs screaming in protest.

Nate thrust his other hand out and grabbed hold of

the flight suit, started dragging his patient backward. Suddenly his burden lessened.

Forcing his eyes open, he found Vance beside him. Unable to speak or dare suck in a breath due to the smoke, Nate pulled with him, finally cleared the blistering heat zone. Vance helped him lift the patient. Nate stepped closer, leaned down so Vance could drape him over Nate's shoulders, and together they hurried away.

Another small explosion went off behind them.

Hurry. Faster. He squinted through the smoke, tried to find a safe path, but it was impossible to see more than six inches in front of him. His lungs burned, screaming from the effort of holding his breath through the exertion.

Four steps later, they gave up the fight. His autonomic nervous system took over, expelling the air in his lungs, greedily sucking in a breath. Nate was powerless to stop it.

He choked, gasped, pulling more smoke in.

No air. Can't breathe.

His foot caught on something, and the added weight of his patient took him down. His knees hit the ground, hard, his spine compressing with a searing pain in his lower back. Nate strangled a cry and maintained his hold on the unconscious man.

Get up. Get up, or you'll die.

He bared his teeth and forced himself upward, struggled to his feet and staggered onward. A gust of wind cleared the smoke a little. Through the inky haze he spotted Vance heading back for him. And behind him, the rest of his teammates, running his way.

Nate shook his head, the only way he could communicate at this point. He didn't want them coming any closer in case—

The ground shook, rolling under his feet as a huge explosion ripped outward.

Nate's gaze was locked on Vance, closest to him but

still too far away to help. His teammate's eyes widened, a look of stunned horror on that dark, smoke-smeared face.

It was the last thing Nate saw. The force of the detonation sent him and his patient airborne. A searing wave of heat blasted over his body, hurtling him headlong into the waiting darkness.

Chapter Seven

Ethan Cruz grunted as the blast wave hit him, throwing him flat on his back in the dirt. Pushing up on his elbows, he shook his ringing head to clear it and looked up. The ringing was still there. He'd been running toward Schroder and Vance when the plane blew. The wreckage was now completely engulfed in flames. And between it and him…

Oh, God, no…

Vance was lying crumpled on his side in the distance, facing toward him. And beyond him, two more bodies were strewn on the ground, one of them Schroder.

He climbed to his feet and took off toward his closest fallen teammate, heart in his throat. Vance wasn't only his best friend, he was the closest thing to a brother Ethan had ever had, and in a few months, would be his brother by marriage. Ethan refused to accept that he might lose him today, shoved down the panic welling inside him and tore across the open space between them.

Even this far from the wreckage the heat was intense,

licking along his skin, the smoke searing his lungs and eyes. Vance wasn't moving. His eyes were closed.

No. You can't fucking be dead. I won't let you.

Ethan grabbed him under the armpits and dragged him away, only stopping when he felt they were at a safe distance from the wreckage. He dropped to his knees beside Vance, grabbed hold of a solid shoulder and got right in his friend's face. "Sawyer. *Sawyer*, can you hear me?"

No response.

Vance's dark brown face was covered in blood, courtesy of a deep laceration in his scalp. The front of his uniform was soaked with blood too. And there was no telling what kind of internal injuries he might have. He and Schroder had been the closest to the explosion, would have taken the brunt of the blast wave.

God dammit. "Sawyer. Come on, you big bastard. Open your eyes and look at me." His voice had a ragged, desperate edge to it that he couldn't control. It terrified him to see his big, tough but laid-back friend lying so still and bloody.

Nothing.

He glanced up as Tuck and Bauer went flying past them toward where Schroder and the crewmember lay. Fuck, this was a nightmare.

Gripping the back of Vance's neck, hard, he bent down so their faces were inches apart. "Vance. You *look* at me, dammit."

The dark eyelids fluttered slightly, and Vance let out a soft moan.

Ethan leaned even closer, pulse drumming in his throat, his stomach a tight knot. "That's right, man. Open your eyes." *Come on. Please.*

Bleary, heavy-lidded deep brown eyes focused on him slowly, full of confusion. And pain. "What…happened?"

"Plane exploded." He eased his grip on the back of his buddy's neck, cupping it now. Holding him steady. "Tell me where you're hurt."

Another deep groan. "Everywhere."

"Your back?"

"Yeah." Vance grimaced, tried to turn onto his back. "Where's Doc?"

"He's being looked after." God, Ethan didn't even know if Schroder was alive. He'd been closer to the plane than Vance when the main explosion happened. But he could only focus on Vance right now, and trust that his other teammates were helping Schroder. "Can you move your hands and feet?"

Vance wiggled them a little, the motion weak and sluggish. "Yeah."

Ethan breathed easier. "Lie still." Footsteps pounded toward them. Seconds later Blackwell and Evers were crouching down next to them. "Need a litter to carry him out on," Ethan said to them.

Evers swiveled his head to search for something. "There's nothing out here but cornstalks. Tuck already called for help a few minutes ago. Crews are coming from the airport right now."

"How long?" Ethan asked, giving Vance a tiny shake when his eyelids began to droop. They had to keep him awake and as alert as possible.

"Another twenty minutes at least."

They couldn't risk moving him again. Vance was far enough away from the fire now to be safe from further injury, and moving him might cause more damage. Better to wait for the paramedics and their backboard in case Vance had a neck, spinal, or internal injury. "Anyone got something to slow this bleeding with?"

"No," Blackwell said, doing a sweep of Vance's body, and ripped open his shirt to expose another deep laceration across his chest. "Vance, can you feel my hands?" he asked, running them down Vance's legs.

"Yeah," he mumbled.

"You hurt anywhere else?" Evers asked, hunkered down behind Vance to bolster him and keep him from turning.

"Not…not sure."

Ethan stripped off his tactical shirt and wrapped it around Vance's head, applying pressure by twisting the ends together while Blackwell did the same to the laceration on Vance's chest.

Vance reached out and took hold of Ethan's arm, staring up at him through swelling eyes. "Don't tell Carm," he groaned.

If it wasn't so freaking serious, Ethan might have laughed. "Don't tell her what?"

"Don't tell her about me." His voice was slurred, sleepy. No doubt due to the major concussion his brain had just withstood. "Not until we know more. She'll…worry."

"I'll wait until we get you outta here," Ethan promised, "but then I gotta call her. I don't want her hearing about this from someone else."

Vance groaned and seemed to sag, his eyes falling closed.

"No, man. You gotta stay awake," Ethan said, giving him a gentle shake.

"Tired," Vance muttered. "Hurts."

Evers leaned over him more. "I know, brother, but you gotta stay with us. You gotta stay awake."

Vance made an irritated sound and seemed to drift off for a moment, only rousing when they shook him and shouted at him. Ethan glanced at his watch, frustration burning through him when he saw that only seven minutes had passed.

Out the corner of his eye he saw Tuck jogging back to them. "Vance," Ethan said to him, giving the side of his face a gentle pat. "Hey, here's Tuck to check on you. Tell him you're okay."

Vance cracked one eye open, the other already swollen shut, and peered up at their team leader as Tuck went down on one knee in front of him. "I'm okay," he murmured, then closed his eye. "Don't let him call Carm."

"What's that?" Tuck asked with a half-smile, trying to keep things light as he laid a fatherly hand on Vance's shoulder.

"Don't want her to worry…"

"I told him I'd wait until we got him safely outta here," Ethan said. "Stubborn bastard." He glanced back at where Bauer still knelt beside Schroder, then shifted his gaze to their team leader, lowering his voice a little. "How's Doc?" He was acutely aware of the intent way Blackwell and Evers were looking at Tuck.

Tuck's brown eyes shifted to his. He didn't say anything. Didn't have to, because the resignation and sadness in his gaze said it all, and the small shake of his head made Ethan's stomach drop.

****

Commander Matt DeLuca strode into the Atlanta Bureau office, eyes on his phone as he scrolled through the various emails he'd missed on the flight up here. He had eight minutes until the meeting with the Atlanta taskforce, and by then he wanted to be up to speed.

The situation out in the mountains was dire. The teenage daughter was confirmed dead. That left only two options: wait the suspect out, or conduct a full-scale breach and clear the place out.

He was a fan of the former. Sending his team into that isolated place against a distraught father ready to kill anyone coming at him was just asking for it, and even if the breach went as planned, there were other lives to consider. One civilian death was inexcusable enough. They needed to defuse the situation first, wait for darkness before carrying out the assault.

As a former Scout/Sniper, Matt couldn't understand how it had happened in the first place. There was no way anyone with that amount of training should ever have mistaken the girl for her father. None. He was bringing in one of his sniper teams for this along with the assaulters on Blue Team, and he had absolute faith in each and every one of them. Because he had personally vetted each and every member.

When he was halfway down the hall to the boardroom, an office door on the left shot open and the Special Agent In Charge of the Atlanta division stepped out, his face showing surprise and then going eerily blank. "Commander. They told me you'd just arrived. I was coming to find you."

Matt lowered his phone, taking in the man's rigid posture and set of his jaw. "What can I do for you?"

"Can you step inside for a minute?" He gestured to his open office.

With apprehension twining through his gut, Matt followed, the sensation growing sharper when the SAIC shut the door and faced him with hands on hips. "There's no easy way to tell you this."

Matt stared at him, bracing himself for bad news. "Tell me what?"

"It's Blue Team. There's been an accident."

"What kind of accident?"

"Their plane went down."

For a second, the words didn't compute. "It *what*?"

The SAIC nodded. "I'm sorry. I don't know much else, but it crashed shortly after takeoff in a rural area a few miles from the airport. Emergency crews are being deployed to the scene as we speak."

Fuck…

It took Matt a moment to speak. "Are there any survivors?"

"I don't know."

Matt immediately raised his phone to call HQ, but it rang in his hand. A wave of relief slammed into him when he saw Tuck's number on screen. "Tuck," he answered, praying there were more than one survivor. "I just heard. Is everyone all right?"

"No."

Matt held his breath, his hand tightening around the phone. "What happened?"

"We'd only been airborne for about twenty seconds or so before something hit us. Not sure what."

Ground fire? A rocket? It didn't make sense. The flight had been arranged at the last minute. How the hell could someone have time to set up and fire that kind of weapon at them, let alone in a restricted area?

"We crashed into a field, managed to get everyone in the back out in time. Schroder and Vance went back for some injured crewmembers. They were caught in the blast wave when the plane exploded."

Matt closed his eyes, his chest tight, lungs like concrete blocks pressing against his ribs. His men were the most critical thing. He'd worry about the cause of the crash later. "Are they alive?"

"Vance is cut up pretty bad, and I'm not sure about internal injuries. He was in and out of consciousness. They're transporting him to the hospital now. As for Doc…" The heavy pause was ominous enough, but Tuck's leaden tone sent a chill up Matt's spine. "I dunno. He's bad. Real bad."

Rubbing at his forehead, Matt tried to process everything. "Is he en route to the hospital now?"

"Yeah. Surgical team is standing by. They'll take him straight to the O.R."

"What about everyone else?"

"Mostly okay, except for the flight crew." Tuck cleared his throat, his voice a little rough, and Matt understood perfectly. It felt like he had a small boulder lodged in his own. "Cruzie just called Carm to let her know about Vance. I was wondering if you wanted me to call Taya, or…" A harsh sigh filled the line. "Doc told us just before we took off that she's pregnant."

Ah, shit. *Shit*. This was fucking heartbreaking. Taya had already been through hell twice before. It was beyond cruel that anything should happen to Nate now. "No. I don't want her to hear it over the phone. I'll have someone go to her."

"Want me to ask Celida to do it?"

"No, I'll handle it." As soon as Celida heard the news, she'd be frantic to get to Tuck. Understandable. "Are you going to the hospital?"

"Yeah, all of us are, just to get checked out, then we'll wait to find out what's going on with the other two."

"I'll be there as soon as I can find a flight. I'll take care of Taya, make sure she gets to the hospital, and meet you there as soon as I can."

"All right. What are you gonna do about the situation in Atlanta?"

"Don't worry about any of that. I'll take care of everything." He'd call SA Grant and have Gold Team deploy there as soon as possible.

Tuck let out a hard exhale. "All right."

"Tuck. You tell the boys I'm coming, okay? I'll be there as soon as I can."

"I will."

Nausea washed over Matt as he disconnected and immediately dialed his wife. His heart slammed against his ribs as it rang, almost bruising. Was this some kind of revenge act? Maybe by Sanchez or the *Venenos*? If someone had brought that plane down, Matt would personally ensure they paid for it dearly.

"Hey, I was just lying in bed thinking about you," Briar murmured, her voice husky with sleep.

"Something's happened," he grated out.

"What's wrong?" Her tone was sharp. Alert.

"Blue Team's plane went down just after takeoff. Vance and Schroder were critically injured. Tuck doesn't know if Schroder will make it."

"Oh, Matt, no."

He drew in a deep breath, locked his jaw for a moment to get himself back under control. "It's a real shitty favor to ask of you, but I need you to go to Taya's right now. I want you to be the one to tell her and take her to the hospital. She's gonna need a friend." He and Briar had been the only ones from the team at Taya and Schroder's wedding. Briar was closer to Taya than she was to any of the other women, and they would all be worried about their guys. It had to be this way.

"Of course," Briar said. No hesitation. No questions. He could hear her already moving around. "I'll be out the door and on my way in five minutes."

"Thanks. I'll be there as soon as I can." He hesitated a second. "One more thing." He rubbed a hand over the back of his neck. "They just found out she's pregnant."

"Oh, man. Okay, I'm on it. See you soon. And, Matt?"

"Yeah?"

"Love you."

He closed his eyes, a sweet ache filling his chest. "I love you too."

Chapter Eight

The chime of the doorbell dragged Taya through the heavy blanket of sleep to consciousness. Blinking, she automatically glanced beside her. But Nathan was gone. She only vaguely remembered him saying goodbye. The early morning light filtering through the edges around the blind told her it was still early. Who would be at their door at this hour?

Grabbing her robe from the foot of the bed, she shrugged it on and dragged herself to her feet, bracing for the inevitable wave of nausea. Early morning seemed to be the toughest for her, when her stomach was empty.

The doorbell rang again.

"Coming," she called out, moving faster. Out of the bedroom and into the hallway, past the living room and kitchen to the entryway. She paused to check through the peephole, surprise jolting through her when she saw Briar standing in the hallway.

Dread congealed in the pit of her stomach as she pulled it open. *Oh, my God. Nathan...* "What's wrong?"

She wouldn't have shown up like this, at this hour, if it wasn't bad.

The other woman regarded her in silence for a moment. "Can I come in?"

Taya folded her arms across her middle, the protective gesture instinctive. "What's happened?" They were friends now, but it had taken months of effort on Taya's part. Briar was slow to trust, and even slower to warm to people. Her coming here like this scared the shit out of Taya.

Briar set a hand on Taya's shoulder and gently turned her around as she stepped inside. "Let's sit down."

Her entire body stiffened, alarm bells blaring in her head. "I don't want to sit down. Tell me what's wrong." *Please let Nathan be alive. Please let him be okay.*

Briar ignored her, kept hold of Taya's upper arm as she steered her toward the living room couch. Taya dropped onto it, her legs stiff, wooden, and stared at the other woman, a hard knot forming in her throat.

Briar met her gaze without flinching, but Taya read the sympathy in those dark eyes. "There's been an accident."

The word echoed in her ears. "What kind of accident?"

"The plane the guys were on hit something shortly after takeoff. It made a crash landing in a field."

Both hands flew to her mouth, horror, terror and denial exploding inside her. She shook her head. "No."

Briar laid a hand on Taya's knee. "The team survived the crash, and evacuated everyone on board. Vance and Nate went back to rescue some crewmembers. There was a big explosion."

Tiny pinpricks needled her skin as the blood drained from her face. "He's not dead." He couldn't be. She couldn't deal with that.

Briar held her gaze, her hand a comforting weight on

Taya's leg. "He was hurt really badly, Taya. They transported him to the hospital. He's undergoing emergency surgery right now."

Nausea swept through her, cold and oily in the pit of her stomach. She shoved to her feet. "I have to get to him," she blurted, and rushed for the bedroom.

Briar was right behind her. "I'll drive you."

Taya didn't answer. Couldn't. Shock and fear clouded everything, and the blockage in her throat increased until she was sucking in ragged gasps. Her hands shook, teeth chattering as she dragged on jeans and a sweater. Her nose and the backs of her eyes burned.

She didn't bother to hide or wipe away the tears as they spilled over. This was the cruelest thing that could ever have happened to her. Losing Nathan would rip her heart out and destroy her soul. And even considering the possibility of their child never knowing his or her father almost brought her to her knees.

But she couldn't think about any of that now. Wouldn't. She had to get to Nathan as soon as possible. He was a fighter. He would fight through this. She would make sure he did.

Briar was standing in the bedroom doorway when Taya came out of the closet. "You ready?"

Taya nodded and rushed past her, pausing only to grab her purse before flying out the door. "What injuries does he have?" she managed once they were driving away from the building.

"I don't know, but it sounds like internal injuries. Head injury, possible brain injury as well. That's all Matt knew when he called. He's flying up here right now."

Taya closed her eyes. *God.* But of course. If Nathan had been caught up in that kind of an explosion, all of that was inevitable. She appreciated that Briar wasn't sugar-coating any of this, instead giving it to her straight. "Did he say what Nathan's chances were?"

"No."

"And Sawyer?"

"He was conscious when they loaded him into the ambulance. I'm not sure if he'll need surgery. The rest of the team was banged up, but from what I understand, nothing too severe."

Just Nathan.

Taya leaned her elbow on the doorframe and covered her mouth with her hand, fighting to hold it together while her mind conjured up nightmarish images of Nathan being blown apart by the explosion. Or burned by the flames.

She swallowed a sob, couldn't stop the hitch in her shoulders.

"I'm so sorry," Briar murmured, skillfully zipping her way in and out of traffic, doing everything she could to get Taya to the hospital as fast as possible.

Unable to answer, Taya nodded. She pictured Nathan on the operating table, his beautiful, strong body torn and burned. Cut open while the surgeons fought to repair the damage to his internal organs. She struggled to remember what she'd said and done before he'd left this morning. Had she kissed him? Told him she loved him?

Time dragged until Briar sped up to the Emergency entrance doors. Taya's fingers were so cold she fumbled to get the seatbelt undone, and by the time she had, Briar was right there, opening the door for her. "Come on. They're all inside waiting for us."

Panic and dread sluiced through her. She didn't think she could take seeing the rest of the team right now, the pity on their faces. Seeing them all healthy while her husband was fighting for his life in the operating room.

Briar took her hand. Taya closed her numb fingers around Briar's, her body on autopilot as she followed the other woman through the large automatic doors.

The musky, slightly sweet smell of the hospital made bile rush into her throat. She swallowed hard, her heart beating like the wings of a frantic, trapped bird beneath her ribs. The overhead lights seemed overly bright, casting a glare over everything.

When they rounded the corner, she stopped dead, her feet refusing to carry her any farther. The low murmur of male voices stopped, everyone falling silent as the five remaining members of Nathan's team stood and faced her.

All five of them were dressed in the same tactical uniforms that Nathan had been wearing when he'd left this morning. All five of their faces streaked with smoke and grime, their uniforms smattered with blood. A few of the women were there as well.

Rachel was pressed into Jake's side, her dark hair mussed, eyes swollen.

Summer had her arms around Adam's waist, her skin blotchy and her nose red.

Celida clung to Tuck's hand.

Zoe stood next to Clay with a serious case of bedhead going on and not a drop of her usual dramatic makeup on, her husband's powerful arm draped over her shoulders in silent comfort.

They all stared at Taya in utter silence. And the weight of all those sympathetic eyes on her was more than she could bear.

A cry of fear and hysteria shot up into her throat. Taya bit it back, somehow kept it from bursting free even though she wanted to scream, wake up from this nightmare.

Tuck stepped forward, his deep brown eyes full of sorrow. "Taya." He lifted a hand as though he would lay it on her shoulder.

Taya retreated a step, unable to stand him touching her. Tuck lowered his hand and didn't say anything. She wrapped her arms around her torso, freezing inside, and found her voice. "Are they still operating?" The words came out hoarse, as though she'd been screaming. And she had been, inside.

He nodded, his face lined with concern. "He's been under for over forty-five minutes now."

So he was still alive. "Did they tell you anything else?"

"No. Nothing yet."

"Was he conscious at all?"

Tuck shook his dark blond head. "I got to him as soon as I could. But he wasn't conscious."

She prided herself on staying calm. On looking at the positive. Except her husband had never fought for his life like this. She'd never been on the verge of losing the man she loved with all hear heart.

Staring into Tuck's sorrowful eyes, she broke. Her face crumpled. She buried it in her hands, at once embarrassed and overcome. Her shoulders jerked, the first hard sob tearing free from between her clenched teeth. It came out ragged. Raw. The cry of a mortally wounded animal.

Strong, yet gentle hands gripped her shoulders and tugged her forward. She was powerless to resist as Tuck drew her to his chest, wrapping her close in his arms. "He's a fighter, Taya," he murmured, his tactical shirt smelling of smoke and sweat. "You know how stubborn he is. And he's going to do everything in his power to pull through this, because he's got you and the baby to live for. He'll fight for you."

He knew about the baby. Nathan must have told them this morning, before boarding the plane.

Taya leaned her forehead on his chest and battled to stem the tears, but it was so hard when her heart was fracturing into a thousand jagged shards of glass.

She became aware of another hand rubbing her back gently, realized Briar was still there. Taya sucked in a shuddering breath and straightened, wiped at her eyes with the heels of her hands. "I want to talk to a doctor," she choked out. She needed to know what was happening, and she needed to know it *now*.

"Okay."

Tuck and Briar steered her over to the row of plastic chairs that lined the hallway wall. Clay's hard face seemed carved from granite when he gently clasped her shoulder as she passed. The others murmured to her, words of sympathy and encouragement, and stepped out of her way. Then Tuck put her into a chair with the promise of bringing back someone to update her on Nathan's condition.

Zoe crouched down in front of her, her turquoise-streaked black hair hanging lank around her shoulders. "Hey, sweetie." She took one of Taya's hands, folded her warmer ones around it gently, and squeezed. "No matter what happens, we're all here for you, okay? Every last one of us."

She forced a tight smile and nodded once. "I know." She appreciated the support and camaraderie. But they couldn't do anything for her. No one could, except the doctors working to save Nathan's life.

It took forever for someone to come talk to her. Briar and Tuck accompanied her into a room where a doctor gave a brief update on Nathan. Saying he was still in surgery where surgeons were trying to repair his collapsed lung, lacerated spleen and liver. No one was entirely sure yet about the severity of the head injury. They would perform more tests once Nathan was in the recovery room.

Assuming he survived the operation.

After the doctor left, Taya leaned her head back against the wall and stared at the closed door, a million turbulent thoughts tumbling through her brain.

Tuck stood and stuffed his hands into his pockets. "Can I get you anything?"

Taya started to shake her head, but Briar interrupted.

"Get her some weak tea and toast or crackers. Maybe some fruit." She lifted a tentative hand to brush a curl away from Taya's face, Tuck already heading out the door. "I bet you're a little sick to your stomach in the mornings now, huh."

Surprised, Taya looked at her. "A little." She rested a hand over her abdomen, striving for at least the semblance of calm. She had to have faith. Be strong.

But she'd never been tested like this before. Not even during her captivity, or the desperate flight through the mountains when she'd escaped. Or that terrifying hostage situation during the Qureshi trial.

Losing Nathan frightened her more than any of that.

"You're shivering. I'll go find you a blanket." Briar stood. "Need anything else?"

"I'm going to call my family. Let them know." She needed to hear her father's and brother's voices.

"Okay. I'll give you some privacy for a bit, but if you need anything, I'll be right outside the door." She jerked her thumb over her shoulder, pointing behind her.

"Thanks."

A few moments later she was alone. In the sterile silence of the empty room, Taya pulled her phone from her purse and dialed her dad. "Dad?" Her voice cracked. She bit her lip, swallowed the tears rushing to the surface once more. "It's Nathan. He's been hurt."

The call ended with her dad promising to get on the next flight there. She called her brother next, but there was no answer. Sometimes he couldn't answer the phone while at work, so she texted him.

After waiting several minutes for him to respond, she sighed and lowered the phone to her lap, leaning her head back and closing her eyes. The fear was still there, the anxiety, but the panic had faded now, leaving a sucking exhaustion in its place.

Her eyes snapped open when the phone vibrated in

her hand. She jerked it from her lap, expecting to see a response from her brother. But it wasn't a Kentucky area code. The number was vaguely familiar though.

I just saw the news. Is he okay? Was he involved?

It took a few seconds for it to hit her. Then realization dawned.

Nathan's sister. She must have seen or heard a story about the crash. The reporter must have mentioned the FBI's Hostage Rescue Team being involved.

Taya bit the inside of her cheek, debating what to do. She'd made the mistake of giving Dara her cell number, not realizing Nathan would have such a harsh reaction to his sister establishing contact. And because Taya hadn't seen any harm in it at the time.

For a moment, she considered deleting the message and blocking the number, because she knew that was what Nathan would want. But something stopped her. Bad history or not, Dara and Nathan were family. The only blood family they had left, now that their mother was gone. Dara at least deserved an answer, to know what was going on.

So Taya did the polite thing and typed out a short response.

No. He's in surgery.

A few seconds passed before the response came back. *Oh, my God. How bad is he?*

About as bad as it could get. *He's fighting for his life.*

She lowered the phone back to her lap, waiting for a reply. It had barely touched her thigh when it began ringing.

Taya stared at the screen, wrestling with her conscience. Her impulse was to answer it, but she held back.

Nathan had been so angry about Dara contacting her. He wasn't the sort of man to cut someone out of his life without good reason, and Dara's behavior about the inheritance after their mother's funeral proved what kind of a person she was. He didn't want her in his life. Didn't want her in Taya's or their baby's life, either. It was so out of character for the loving man she knew, Taya had to respect it, even if she wished his relationship with Dara was different.

Her resolve hardened. She declined the call, and sent another message instead. *I'll let you know what happens.*

The phone rang again, the ring somehow more urgent this time. Almost annoyed. Again, Taya didn't answer, and this time she didn't feel bad about ignoring it.

Finally a text came back. *Tell him I'll call him once he's better.*

Taya blinked in shock, then stared at the screen in utter disbelief. Was that it? No, *I'm pulling for him/praying for him*, or *please tell him I love him despite the distance between us*. No offer to travel there as soon as possible, as her father was doing right now. As her brother would as soon as he heard the news. No words about wanting to see him, to be there for him.

And then it hit her, with all the force of a sucker punch to the stomach.

Dara wasn't worried about him dying, didn't care if he did. No, she was worried he would die and leave the unsettled issue of the inheritance—a small amount of money Nathan didn't give a rat's ass about anyway—with Taya listed as the beneficiary of all his assets.

She didn't give a shit about her brother or what he was going through right now, what sort of recovery or maybe diminished life he faced if he pulled through this. She just wanted the fucking money.

It was the most disgusting, damning evidence Dara could have given.

And there was no goddamn way Taya would let that kind of poison touch their lives ever again.

Rage burned through the fear, obliterated the helplessness. Setting her jaw, she typed back her final message. *Don't bother. And don't contact either one of us ever again.*

As soon as she hit send, she blocked the number, instantly feeling stronger. More in control.

Resting a hand to her belly, she sent a silent message of comfort and reassurance to the fragile being tucked deep inside her body. She had a family of her own to protect now: her husband and their unborn child. She would protect them with all of her strength, until the last breath left her body.

They were everything. And next to that, nothing else mattered.

Chapter Nine

Carmela burst through the hospital's main entrance with her hair a wet, tangled mess, wearing the first top and pair of jeans she'd found in the closet, and a terrible sense of déjà vu stalking her. This was like Miami all over again, rushing to the hospital while not knowing if one of the most important men in her life was dead or alive.

Only this time, it was *the* most important man in her life.

Thirty seconds out of the shower, getting ready to go pick her mom up at the airport, she'd gotten the call from her brother. His words had hit her like a shockwave.

You need to get up here to the hospital. Our plane crashed. Sawyer's hurt bad.

She didn't even remember the drive here, barely remembered her frantic call to her mom, who was on a plane heading up here right now. She wasn't even sure her mom would be able to understand the message she'd left, her voice had been unrecognizable, even to her. *Mom, the team's been in a plane crash. Sawyer's hurt bad. I'm heading to the hospital now.*

All she knew was Sawyer had been caught in the blast when the plane exploded. No one knew how extensive or severe his injuries were.

God, she couldn't believe she'd been so annoyed with him yesterday about his lack of enthusiasm over the wedding plans. What the hell did it all matter now? She'd been so caught up in the details, wanting her own way, pushing him on each point to get him to agree when she knew damn well he didn't want any of it.

She felt sick over it, and also that she hadn't taken the time to say a proper goodbye before he'd walked out their door this morning. The terror of losing him had wiped all the unimportant things away, showing her what really mattered. She only hoped she got to make amends and honor his feelings the way she should have all along.

Frantic to get to him, she flew around the corner and almost barreled into a wide chest. Strong hands caught her, steadied her, and she jerked her head up, looking into eyes the exact same golden brown as hers.

Her throat closed up. "*Ethan.*"

Her brother gathered her into a tight hug, his chin resting on the top of her head. "Hey, hon."

She set her hands flat on his chest and pushed, meeting his eyes. He had little nicks on his left cheek and his face was streaked with grime and smoke, but otherwise he seemed fine. She shoved that worry aside and focused solely on Sawyer. "What's happening? How is he?"

"He's gonna be okay."

Carmela stopped breathing for an instant, searching his eyes. Was he lying? People always said things like that when they were trying to calm someone down. Break it to them gently. "You better not be lying to me right now." She'd never forgive him if he was.

"I'm not. He's awake and talking. That's great news. I don't know anything else, the staff kicked me out of the treatment area while they were looking at him. They took him down for x-rays and a CT scan."

Relief hit her so hard she sagged, her knees melting like hot candle wax. Ethan caught her with a muttered curse and held her tighter. "You swear?"

"I swear."

"I want to see him." She had to, before she lost her mind with worry. She wouldn't believe Sawyer was going to be okay until she saw him with her own eyes. And *going* to be okay was not the same as *being* okay. Did he have broken bones? A concussion? Did he need surgery of some sort? Not being able to be there with him when he was injured and in pain was like a knife in her chest, slowly twisting.

Ethan rubbed a hand up and down her back. "I know. I'll take you up as soon as they give us the okay."

She expelled a deep sigh, cleared her head. "How's Schroder doing?"

Ethan's entire face tightened. "Still in surgery, last I heard. It doesn't look good."

"Poor Taya. Has she got anyone with her?"

"Yeah, Briar."

Carmela leaned back to stare at him, raising her brows. "Briar?" She'd been a loner for so long, even social get togethers like last night's barbecue were still hard for her. Not that Briar would ever admit it. Probably not even under torture. That woman was as tough as they came, just one of the things Carmela admired about her.

Her brother nodded. "Rest of the team is waiting down there too." He ran a hand over the back of his neck. "Just before takeoff, Schroder told us Taya's pregnant."

"Oh," she breathed, covering her mouth with one hand. "Oh, that's just so sad..."

"Yeah, this fuckin' sucks."

She shook her head, trying to take it all in. "What the hell happened, anyway?"

"Nobody knows yet. Sounded like we were taking ground fire. Bam-bam-bam-bam-bam, all these impacts hitting us just after takeoff. I doubt anyone was shooting at us, so the only other possibility that makes sense are multiple bird strikes in the props that got sucked into the engines or something."

Ethan took her to a small lounge off the main hallway where his fiancée, Marisol, was waiting. As soon as they walked in Soli jumped up and embraced Carmela. "You okay?" her friend asked her.

Carmela squeezed her hard. "Much better than I was for the past half an hour, yeah. Where's everybody else?"

"In another waiting room with Taya."

"Ah. God, poor Taya."

"Yeah."

Ethan pressed a cup of hot coffee into her hands. Together they sat killing time, watching the minutes tick past on the clock beside the door as they waited for word on Sawyer's condition.

Carm's phone rang with her mother's distinctive ringtone. "Hi, *Mami*," she answered, and immediately got a barrage of frantic Spanish in her ear. "I haven't seen him yet, they're still doing tests." She paused while her mother launched into another worried burst of words, did what she could to calm her. "Yes, Ethan's fine. I'm sitting with him and Soli right now."

Ethan and Marisol were both watching her as she hung up a few minutes later. "She's coming straight here from the airport," Carm told them, then added to Ethan, "And you're on her shit list for not answering your phone—"

She broke off when the door opened and a nurse poked her head in. "You must be Agent Vance's family."

Carmela shot to her feet. "Yes. I'm his fiancée."

The nurse nodded and gestured for her to come toward the door. "He's up in his room now. All the tests are done and we're just waiting for the results. He's conscious and alert, which are both good signs. You can go up and see him if you want."

"*Yes*." She barely refrained from bulldozing the nurse over on her way into the hall, Ethan and Soli right behind her.

Her heart thudded against her ribs as they rode up to the fourth floor and started down another hallway. Trepidation twined inside her, tying her stomach in knots. She was desperate to see Sawyer, but afraid of what she'd find. They'd been on the cusp of making their dreams come true by getting married. This would impact everything.

She drew herself up, raised her chin. When she walked into that room she was not going to fall apart. She would be strong for him. Stand by him no matter what happened.

The nurse paused before a door and gave a sympathetic smile. "He might be a little groggy from the medication."

"That's okay." As long as he knew she was there and could respond, that's all that mattered to her right now.

Turning the corner, she held her breath. Beneath the thin blanket covering the bed, the outline of feet came into view. Her gaze traveled up the legs, to the strong arms, an IV taped to one of them, and finally up to his face.

She smothered a gasp, fought to hold it together, and approached the bed. His eyes were swollen shut, the bruising all around them evident even with his dark skin. He had a line of stitches that extended down the left side of his scalp that veered over to his forehead. A bandage started at the top of his sternum and disappeared beneath the light blue gown he wore.

God, he looked like he'd gone a dozen, bare knuckle

rounds with a heavyweight fighter.

Standing beside him, gazing down at that poor, ravaged face she wanted to kiss all over, she curled her hand around his, aware of Ethan and Marisol hovering near the foot of the bed. "Sawyer? Baby, I'm here. Can you hear me?"

His eyelids twitched, a frown pulling at his eyebrows as his head slowly turned toward her. "Car…Carm?" His voice was hoarse.

Tears flooded her eyes, but a smile stretched her lips. She cupped his right cheek with her free hand, pressed his scraped and bloody knuckles to her lips. "Yeah. I'm here."

WHATEVER THEY'D GIVEN him had knocked him on his ass and made everything fuzzy.

Sawyer tried to force his heavy, swollen eyelids apart, his face angled toward that beautiful, familiar voice. Managing to open his eyes a slit, he squinted up into Carmela's gorgeous, worried face. "Hey." He even attempted a smile for her.

She pressed his hand to her cheek and leaned over him, the scent of her shampoo and perfume wrapping him in comfort. "Hi. How are you feeling?"

"I'm good." Actually, he felt like a five-ton truck had run over him. "Can still move my legs and arms."

"That's good."

"Yeah." There was someone standing at the foot of his bed. He squinted harder, made out Ethan's drawn face, and Marisol beside him. "Hey, brother."

Ethan stepped forward to clasp his hand, squeezed tight. "Good to see you, man."

He focused on the woman at his side. "Hey, Soli."

She shot him a relieved smile. "Hi, Sawyer. You gave us all one hell of a scare."

"Yeah, you did," Carmela murmured, leaning down

to kiss his forehead. "God, you're a mess."

"Nah, I'm all right." He cleared his throat, emotion threatening to overwhelm him. His best friend and fiancée were on either side of him, each holding one of his hands. Anchoring him in his confusion.

His family. And they would never abandon him, no matter what. He swallowed hard, trying to force his throat open. Christ, what were they pumping into him that was making him this way?

He turned his head to the left, focused on Ethan. "What happened?"

His friend's face shuttered. "You and Schroder went back to help some wounded crewmembers, and the plane exploded."

Sawyer didn't remember that. There were only little snippets. The last one of Ethan's face hovering directly over his, his expression urgent as he talked to him. *Hold on, Saw. You gotta hold on for me, brother.* "How's Doc?"

Ethan's jaw tightened and he squeezed Sawyer's hand. "He's still in surgery. But it… It doesn't look good."

Aww, shit, no. Not Doc. Not him, and not now that he had a baby on the way.

"Everybody else is waiting with Taya downstairs," Carm said to him, her thumb gliding gently over his cheek. "We just have to stay positive, hope for the best."

"What about you, buddy? You in pain?" Ethan asked.

"Not too bad." He hurt fucking everywhere, but the headache was unlike anything he'd ever felt before. Even the light hurt. "Docs said I didn't break anything, just rung my bell really good."

"So no surgery?" Carm asked, an anxious note in her voice. He felt bad that she'd had such a scare, that she'd been so worried.

"Naw. Unless they found something bad on my scans."

"Your poor eyes," she whispered, kissing his forehead again.

"Hey, at least they still work. Just a little swollen, is all." And so was his tongue, apparently, because his words sounded slurred, even to his own ears. God, what a bitch of a day, and he hoped like hell that Schroder battled through this. Everyone would be gutted if they lost him.

The realization of how close he'd come to death today settled over him like a suffocating fog. He pushed it all back and focused on the positive, so damn glad to have Carm and Ethan here.

Carmela leaned over to rest her forehead against his gently. "Baby, I'm so sorry that I pushed you about the wedding."

The guilt in her voice made him frown. "What? No, it's okay—"

"No, it's not, and I feel awful about it now." She tucked her face into the curve of his neck, the caress of her hair against his face soothing. "I don't care about venues, how many people are there, or menus, or stupid flower arrangements. I just want to marry you. So if you still want something small, then we'll do something small."

Sawyer tugged his hand free and reached up to slide it into the thick fall of her hair. "I love you."

She pressed closer, seeking comfort as much as he drank it in from her. "God, I love you too."

Exhaustion began to creep through his body. Carmela and Ethan's lowered voices murmured somewhere in the background, growing more distant by the second. He allowed his eyes to close completely and let himself drift, both his hands held by two of the people he loved most.

The next thing he knew he jerked awake as a stream

of breathless Spanish hit him from over by the doorway. He forced his eyes open, still couldn't see much through the tiny gap between the lids. Ethan and Marisol were gone but Carm was still beside him. She was looking toward the door with a deep frown, and shaking her head.

"*Mami*, shhh, you'll wake him," she admonished in a whisper.

Mami?

Sawyer jerked his shuttered gaze toward the door. The sight of the woman standing there made his heart turn over and caused a huge grin to spread across his face. "Mama Cruz," he mumbled, his tongue feeling like it was made of cotton.

Chest heaving as she panted, out of breath as though she'd just run a mile, Mama Cruz let out a sob and rushed at him, practically shoving her daughter out of the way to get to his bedside.

Two plump, surprisingly strong arms wound around his neck, and a pair of lips dropped kisses over his forehead and cheeks. "Sawyer. *Ai, mi hijo*." She gulped back a sob and kept babbling in rapid-fire Spanish, a litany of relief and gratitude he only caught snippets of.

Still grinning, Sawyer lifted a hand to pat her back. "I'm okay, Mama." Shit, this woman melted him faster than ice cream on a hot Oklahoma summer day. It had only been him and his strict, hard-ass father growing up. Having this big-hearted woman accept him as her own son meant the world to him.

"You are not okay," she retorted in her adorable accent, displaying more of that Puerto Rican fire that he so loved about her and Carm.

She pulled back and framed his face with her small hands, gave him a watery smile. "But you will be. Carmelita and I will see to it." She straightened, determination stamped into every loveable feature. "Now. What do we need to do to get you more comfortable, ah?

You want your bed adjusted maybe? Some food? Or maybe a quick wash, hm?" She yanked down the sleeve of her sweater and started rubbing at the side of his face, an annoyed scowl creasing her forehead. "You are filthy. I can't believe they wouldn't at least clean you up."

The sleeve must not have worked, because she scowled harder and licked her finger before rubbing at something on his face.

Mom spit. So gross, but it was so damn endearing that she would treat him as one of her own, he didn't care.

The thought of her giving him a sponge bath made him cringe inside. He loved her to death, but he didn't want her seeing him naked. "No, I'm fine for now—"

"Ach!" She thrust a warning finger at him, that stern look on her face that told him not to argue. Without waiting for a response she turned to Carmela, who was unsuccessfully trying to hide a smile. "You go get the nurse, so we can get our boy what he needs."

"No, there's a call button right here," Carm said, reaching for it.

Her mother leveled that same warning finger at her, one eyebrow cocked in a silent command anyone who knew her would recognize instantly. Resistance was futile. Way easier to just do as she said, and then no one got hurt. "Don't say to me no." She clapped her hands, waved them at the door in a shooing motion. "Go. Go, go."

Carm sighed, got up and did as she was told.

When it was just the two of them, Sawyer laid there and said nothing as Mama Cruz fussed with his bed, raising the head and feet until she deemed it was perfect, then fluffed his pillow and settled it beneath the back of his neck.

All the while he thanked his blessings for being alive and whole…and prayed for his teammate who was battling for his life somewhere downstairs right now.

Chapter Ten

He's going to wake up once they lower the dosage. He's going to be fine.

Taya kept repeating the words over and over as she sat by Nathan's intensive care unit bedside, holding his hand. After an agonizing six-hour wait, they'd finally let her come see him once he was out of recovery. The number of monitors and machines he was hooked up to frightened her, as did the sluggish beep of the heart monitor. His heart beat seemed way too slow to her.

One surgeon had told her it was a miracle Nathan survived the operation at all. They'd transfused him twice due to blood loss. The damage to his spleen had been so catastrophic they'd elected to remove it entirely, along with one-fifth of his liver. As it was, they were keeping him in a medically induced coma to allow his body to begin healing.

Even if the liver was capable of regenerating, it didn't make Taya feel better about Nathan's chances. Because the head injury was the wild card in this scenario.

He hadn't been wearing a helmet at the time of the explosion. The ECGs and CT scans had shown both significant coup and countercoup lesions in both his frontal and occipital lobes, due to the force of the explosion and his impact with the ground. A neurologist was reviewing the data now and would come talk to her when he had more information.

So yet again, she was playing the waiting game.

Her heart broke a little more as she brushed a damp lock of hair away from his forehead. His face was bruised, his eyes slightly swollen but other than that he looked so peaceful, like he was only resting. She kept waiting for him to open his eyes and look at her. If he could just do that, she'd breathe easier. Why had he gone back to get those wounded men? If he hadn't, he might be okay right now. And both airman had died of their injuries anyway, so it was all for nothing.

As soon as she thought it she reprimanded herself. Nathan was a former PJ. Running into danger to help someone else was hardwired into him. That bravery, that selflessness that had put him in this situation were also two of the qualities she loved and admired most about him. Even if he'd known what would happen, he still would have tried to save those crewmen.

A soft knock came at the door. Taya half-turned toward it. "Come in."

It cracked open, revealing both Tuck and Matt. "We just wanted to check on you guys," Matt said softly. He was dressed for meetings, wearing a suit instead of his tactical uniform and Chargers cap. His pale blue dress shirt was wrinkled and rumpled, completely unlike him.

"Please, come in." She straightened, gave them a tired smile as they approached to stare down at Nathan.

"Has his status changed at all?" Tuck asked.

"No. They're going to keep him in the coma for at least the next few days to let him rest and heal. Then they'll do more tests and go from there."

But the odds weren't good. 60/40 he wouldn't survive the next forty-eight hours, and 70/30 he'd have some degree of permanent disability if he did. She tried not to think of the numbers. The doctors didn't know how strong her husband was. She did.

Nathan could beat those odds. She was going to make sure he did.

"Well he's been through a lot. Give him a little time to get on the mend, and he'll come around," Matt said, then crossed to her and laid a hand on her shoulder. "So. How are you holding up?"

Taya chewed on the inside of her cheek, appreciating that he cared. She'd been wrestling with herself for hours, trying to think of all the possible outcomes she might face in an effort to prepare herself. "To tell you the truth, I'm not sure which scares me the most—him not waking up at all, or the possibility of him waking up with permanent brain damage."

Neither man said anything in response, but Matt squeezed her shoulder. "It's never a bad thing to be prepared, just in case, but we all have to stay positive. And Tuck told me the news earlier. About the baby. Congratulations."

She peered up at his handsome face, met his bright green eyes. They held kindness and concern. "Thank you. I'm trying not to worry too much, for the baby's sake. But it's hard." Impossible, more like.

"Yeah. But try and remember how much he's got to live for. He'll fight for you and the baby with everything he's got."

"I know." He wouldn't leave them willingly.

Removing his hand from her shoulder, he set both on his hips and studied Nathan, his demeanor calm, comforting. "He looks a lot better than I expected him to, all things considered."

"Still my hottie," Taya murmured with a half-smile that made Matt grin.

"Have you talked to your dad?"

"Yes. He and my brother are both flying up to stay with me for a while."

"That's good."

"Yes." She couldn't wait for them to get here. "Do you know yet what caused the crash?"

"Airport radar confirmed something hit the right inner prop just after takeoff. We think it was a large remote-control drone. It damaged the prop, but the lithium battery probably exploded on impact. The debris damaged the second prop and the wing, maybe severed the fuel line, and that could have caused an explosion."

"A drone," she repeated. "You mean like, someone's toy? Or a weapon someone was trying to sabotage their flight with?"

"As of right now there's nothing to indicate it was anything but a tragic accident with a civilian drone. The flight was arranged last minute. Anyone looking to target us wouldn't have had time to plan anything. It was just a freak accident. And whoever was operating the drone shouldn't have been flying it anywhere near the base. It's restricted airspace. Investigators are looking for leads. When they find the person, charges will be laid."

Charges weren't going to bring her husband back.

Taya shook her head. Unbelievable. Someone flying his toy drone before the crack of fucking dawn near a runway had caused all of this. And if Nathan's plane had taken off either a few seconds earlier or later, none of this would have happened. How sadly ironic that after all he'd done and all the harrowing missions he'd undertaken, a civilian drone had done this to him.

"What about the mission they were supposed to do?" When Nathan woke up, he would want to know.

"Gold Team is handling it," Matt said. "I'll be

heading to Atlanta in the morning, but you can reach me anytime on my cell."

For some reason, the thought of him leaving made her feel even more alone. Maybe because Nathan worshipped and looked up to him so much. Almost like a father figure. "Thank you."

"Taya, you need anything?" Tuck asked from the foot of the bed.

She tried to remember the last thing she'd eaten. Some crackers, fruit and a little bit of tea. No wonder her stomach was growling so bad. "I am kinda hungry."

"I'll get you something. What do you feel like?"

"Some soup maybe? And crackers?" She sighed. "I'd love a decaf or herbal tea, too, if they have any." Something hot, to warm her from the inside out, melt the icy fear that had formed in the pit of her belly.

"I'll find some. Maybe I'll get a double portion, and some snacks to keep you going, since you're eating for two now."

She forced a little smile. "Yes."

Tuck's gaze cut to Nathan, then back to her. He gestured toward the bed. "May I?"

"Of course." She wanted them to acknowledge Nathan. Talk to him. Maybe he could still hear them and they just didn't realize it.

Tuck rounded the other side of the bed, stood looking down at Nathan for a long moment, then took Nathan's right hand and spoke in a low, clear voice, his southern drawl soothing her as much as his words did. "Doc, it's Tuck. Just wanted to say the boys and I are all thinking about you. We need you, brother. So you go on and take all the time you need to heal up, but you gotta get better. And we'll look after your lady until you can do it yourself."

Taya's eyes burned with an unexpected rush of tears. "I appreciate that, thank you."

Both Tuck's and Matt's gazes snapped to her. "You're both family to us all," Matt said. "And we take care of our family."

She broke eye contact because it was simply too overwhelming to hold it, and because her throat was now clogged. "Thanks." It was barely a whisper, but it was important to her that they know how much she appreciated their support and kindness. Everyone had been so wonderful to her since she'd gotten together with Nathan, from the guys, to Matt and Briar, and all the female significant others.

"How are the others?" she asked Matt.

"Vance is all settled in his room two floors down. They're keeping him in for at least another few days, for observation. Carm and her mom are with him. The others just left a little while ago. They were all hanging around downstairs waiting for word on Doc. They wanted to see him, but Tuck and I had a hard enough time getting permission to come in here, so I told everyone to go home and said I'd update them if anything changed. I didn't want them all coming up here at once, but the boys will be stopping in to visit Nate on a rotating basis." He paused, studying her. "If that's all right with you."

She appreciated him checking. "Yes, absolutely. And it would mean a lot to Nathan."

"Well, he means a lot to all of us." Again those clear green eyes met hers. "And so do you, Taya. We're here for you too, no matter what."

She bit her lip and nodded, swallowing the tears.

"I'm gonna go grab you some food," Tuck said, backing toward the door. "Back in a bit."

As soon as the door swung shut behind him, Matt took Tuck's place to stand on the other side of Nathan's bed. "You keep fighting, Doc," he told Nathan, gripping her husband's limp hand in his. "Just keep fighting." He straightened and shifted his gaze to her, still holding

Nathan's hand. "You must be tired."

She nodded. "I'm beat." Physically, mentally, emotionally. She was drained to the point of feeling hollow inside. But she'd been too keyed up with worry to risk falling asleep. What if Nathan woke or needed her, and she missed it?

"You staying the night?" Matt asked her.

"*Oh,* yeah. I'm not leaving his side until he wakes up." She wanted to crawl onto the bed with Nathan, lie close to him and put her head next to his on the pillow, but he'd just had a major life-saving operation and she was scared of bumping or jostling him in her sleep. So the dreaded pullout chair it was.

Matt nodded as though unsurprised, then glanced around the tiny room and frowned. "I'll see if I can get a small inflatable or foam mattress in here for you. Those pullout chairs are like sleeping on a short plywood board."

They really were. "I'd love that, thank you."

He focused on her again. "It's nothing. Whatever you need, we'll get it for you. And you don't have to stay here all the time. If you decide you need a break, take it. One of us will always be here to sit with him, and that's a promise."

She moaned and covered her eyes with one hand. "I've been doing such a good job of holding it together, but you're gonna make me cry."

His low chuckle floated through the air, warm as a hug. "No shame if you do. I won't tell anyone."

She loved him dearly. All of them. And to help him pull through and beat the odds, Nathan needed all the support and encouragement he could get.

Matt was as good as his word. After Tuck brought her a tray of food, both men left and reappeared under an hour later with an inflatable mattress, complete with bedding. They not only set it up for her, but Matt literally tucked her in, too, arranging the blankets around her.

Then he crouched down next to her and smoothed a hand over her hair. "You've got my number?"

"Yes."

He nodded once. "If you need anything, or if there's a change in his status, call."

"I will."

"I'll come by in the morning. Try to get some sleep." He laid a hand on the top of her head, his expression full of admiration and tenderness. "No wonder he calls you Little Warrior." Squeezing her shoulder gently, he rose to his feet and switched off the light on his way out of the room.

She spent a fitful night on the floor next to her husband, reaching up for his still hand in the darkness, letting the beep of the heart monitor reassure her that he was still with her. Time dragged, the hours blurring, but he survived the first forty-eight hours. Then seventy-two. And ninety-six. And still the doctors kept him in the coma.

Over the next nine days she became intimately familiar with the hospital routine. Nurses came and went at all hours to check Nathan's vitals, check his catheter, adjust his medication levels or draw blood. Within a few days she knew pretty much every nurse working in the ICU, and greeted them by name whenever they came to tend to Nathan.

A doctor stopped by once in the morning just after breakfast, and again before dinner. Sometimes it was one of the surgeons who had operated on Nathan. Sometimes it was a thoracic specialist or a neurologist. None of them had anything useful or hopeful to offer. Every day, the same verdict.

Nathan was surviving, but he wasn't improving.

Her dad and brother were godsends, keeping her fed, letting her nap while they kept watch over Nathan. She refused to leave the hospital, using earplugs when she absolutely needed sleep. Nathan's teammates came in every day, three of them arriving for a fifteen-minute shift at regularly spaced intervals that didn't interfere with the nurses or Taya's sleep schedule.

The women came too, checking on her and bringing her little treats or things to make her stay more comfortable. A pair of fluffy slippers and a memory foam pillow. Pink flannel jammies with little black skulls on them from Zoe. Flowers and chocolates, an electric kettle, mug and collection of herbal teas. Books and magazines. It was all so thoughtful and overwhelming, to be looked after like that.

And yet…

Even with such a solid support system behind her and around her, after the first ten days came and went without any change, she began to lose hope. She didn't dare tell anyone or let it show, but the guilt was terrible.

Then, on day eleven, the doctors decided it was time to wean Nathan off his meds. They'd removed the staples from his chest and abdomen. His skin had healed. Now it was time to see if his brain had as well.

Taya remained perched at his side over the next three days, waiting and praying for an uptick in brain activity. For him to wake up, open his eyes. Anything.

But nothing happened.

On night fifteen, dispirited and crushed, she changed into her pink and black bat-print pajamas and crawled into her makeshift bed on the floor beside Nathan's bed while her father hovered over her, his face lined with concern.

"Sweetie, you sure you don't want to go home for a while tonight? You're done in, you should see the circles under your eyes. I'll stay with Nathan. If anything changes I'll call you right away."

"No, but thanks. I promised him I wouldn't leave him."

Her dad sighed and stuffed his hands into his

pockets. "You sure?"

"Yes." There was no conviction or heat behind the word. She was too damn exhausted to argue, too numb to expend another ounce of energy.

When the beeping started to quicken, she assumed she was dreaming. Then her eyes popped open, and every muscle seized as Nathan's heart rate began to pick up. Taya shoved into a sitting position and stared at his profile in the dimness. "Nathan?"

The beeping stayed steady. Taya rose and took his hand, leaned over him to peer into his face. "Nathan, can you hear me?" He didn't react. The increase in heart rate had to be a positive sign, right?

What if it means the opposite?

She hurried around the other side of the bed, flipped on the bedside light and grabbed for the call button, her hands unsteady. Shit, was he going into cardiac arrest or something?

The plastic device was cold in her hand as she slid her thumb over top of the button.

The sheets rustled.

Taya smothered a gasp and jerked her gaze to her husband. "Nathan?" She leaned over him, grabbed his hand and squeezed. "*Nathan.*"

His eyelids flickered. They *flickered*.

She held her breath, waiting. Praying.

Please, baby. Please wake up and look at me.

A slight frown twitched across his forehead. And then those beautiful, familiar hazel eyes flipped open and peered up at her.

Chapter Eleven

Nate woke to utter confusion. It felt like he was trapped deep beneath the water, the weight pushing him down, making his limbs sluggish as he swam toward the surface.

He clawed his way toward it, fighting through layer after layer. Then he realized the smothering sensation was because he couldn't breathe right. And the pain. The pain made him want to go back under, escape. But something told him he had to surface now, or he would drown.

Someone was calling him. He headed for it. Held onto it and used it as beacon in the heavy darkness.

The nearer he got to the surface, the worse the pain got. His body tensed, recoiling from the pain.

His head pounded like someone was driving a steel spike into it, his chest and abdomen were on fire, and every breath hurt. But he knew that voice. That sweet, gentle voice coming from next to him.

He opened his eyes in the darkness, searching for her. "T…Taya," he ground out.

"Yes. Yes, I'm here," she said with a half-sob.

He was too weak to even turn his head toward her. Searing agony knifed his insides. He shallowed his breathing, concentrated on her voice. The sadness in it alarmed him even more.

That Taya was near tears told him it had to be bad. *Really* fucking bad. Jesus, was he dying?

She pressed her cheek to his, cupped his other one in her palm while he ran through the areas that hurt. He could move his hands and feet, but he couldn't remember the names of the parts that were sorest, except his head. Why was everything so foggy?

The sweet, spicy combination of vanilla and cinnamon filled his nostrils, calming his galloping heart a little. "What…"

"Are you in pain?"

He tried to nod. Instantly regretted it as pain shot up his neck and through his skull, stealing his breath.

"Shh, just lie still," she murmured, gently stroking his hair now. "Do you remember the crash?"

Crash? "Mmm mmm." It hurt to talk. Hurt to *think*.

"Your team was involved in a plane crash. Everyone survived, but you went back to help some wounded crewmen. There was an explosion. They had to operate on you to repair your lung and liver, and removed your spleen. You had a really bad concussion too. You've been asleep since it happened over two weeks ago."

Oh, shit.

He closed his eyes and tried to concentrate, to remember. A plane? They must have been headed out on a mission or training op. Why couldn't he remember?

Little fragments came back to him. Flashes of memory. Him holding Taya in his lap at the team barbecue at DeLuca's place. She'd fallen asleep with her dinner in her hands. He'd been angry about something on the way home. Then he'd been packing. He'd stood in their bedroom looking down at Taya curled up asleep in their bed. Marveling at her because—

The baby. They were having a baby.

His heart thudded harder as he tried to remember what happened after that. But there was nothing else. Not even a glimmer. Only a blank wall.

"It's okay, the doctors said some short-term memory loss was inevitable. And they've got you on a lot of different meds right now." Taya stroked his hair again. "I'm just so glad you're awake and talking to me, and that you can move." Relief was heavy in her voice.

He was still trying to process all of that, wrap his mind around it, when the noise in the room increased. Taya remained where she was as other people came in with rapid footsteps. Moments later people were poking him, prodding him, asking questions that all blurred together.

Nate clamped his back teeth together, fighting the urge to yell at them to shut the hell up. He hurt all over, he was scared to death, and just wanted his wife. Needed to see and feel her.

Cutting through all the noise and motion around him, he reached out a hand for Taya. "Turn on the light," he managed. "Want to see you."

Everything went quiet. A sudden, deafening silence filled the room, as if they'd been placed inside a giant vacuum and all sound had been sucked out of the room.

Taya's cool hand closed around his, her slender fingers squeezing tight. "Nathan… The light *is* on."

The words hit him like a sledgehammer to the chest, forcing all the air from his lungs, a crushing pressure clamping around his aching ribs.

A bolt of sheer terror forked through him, sending a wave of ice through his body.

Oh, my God, I'm blind.

Chapter Twelve

"Okay, *Mami*. We'll see you in another few weeks."

Sawyer covered a grin as Carm hugged her mother goodbye on the sidewalk out front of the airport. She loved her mom to pieces, but after this latest extended visit due to Sawyer's recovery, she was glad to put her mom on a plane.

And as much as Sawyer adored his future mother-in-law, he was looking forward to being alone with Carm again. Having Mama Cruz stay with them for so long had put a total damper on their sex life.

Ethan and Marisol took their turns saying goodbye next. Then Mama Cruz turned to Sawyer, a sad, loving smile on her face.

"Sawyer." She held her plump arms out expectantly. He adjusted his Stetson so the brim wouldn't hit her in the face as he leaned down and pulled her into a hug. His heart squeezed at the way she held onto him, the top of her head barely reaching the center of his chest. So tiny, but every molecule of her was made of love. "You keep getting better, you hear?"

"Yes, ma'am."

One more squeeze, a pat on the back, and Mama Cruz let him go to peer up at him with eyes the exact same golden-brown shade as her children's. "You won't rush things. You'll do as the doctors say?"

"No. And yes."

She turned her attention to her daughter. "And you. You'll make sure he eats properly, yes?"

To her, eating properly meant serving him at least three home cooked meals every day. She'd seen to it personally ever since he came home from the hospital. He'd put on seven pounds already, helped along by all the batches of homemade brownies and his favorite caramel flan she knew he couldn't get enough of. And since he was still recovering, she'd made it plain she now expected Carm to take over on her behalf now that she was leaving.

Sawyer was the first to admit he loved the way Mama Cruz spoiled him, and he even found her bossiness endearing, because it meant she cared so much. Carm didn't see it that way though.

His fiancée gave a dramatic sigh. "Mom, *please*. Give it a rest."

Her mother raised both eyebrows at her. "He's the one who needs a rest. You need to take care of him."

Out of the corner of his eye, Sawyer noticed Ethan covering his mouth with a fist, trying to cover up a laugh with a cough. He failed spectacularly.

Carm aimed an exasperated look at their mother. "I *will* take care of him, but I don't think making himself a sandwich now and again is going to set him back any. Or if he doesn't get his daily helping of flan," she added in a blasé tone.

"But do you really want to take that chance?" Sawyer asked her, only half-teasing. He *loved* that flan.

All the lacerations and bruises were healed up now, with the exception of a little bit in his brain. The strict concussion protocol the doctors had him on dictated that he had at least another month of recovery left before he could begin training and rejoin his team, and that might not even be until after the wedding and honeymoon, depending on how things went. Until then, two new guys were filling in for him and Schroder, who might not ever be able to return.

That was so damn horrifying, Sawyer tried not to think about it.

Carm elbowed him in the ribs. "Quiet."

"And you'll keep taking the pills I bought you?" Mama Cruz asked him.

He hid a grimace. They were some godawful concoction of ingredients she'd found in a Puerto Rican specialty store up here that were supposed to help him heal faster and get rid of the last of the bruising in his brain. Sawyer was convinced she'd bought them from a witch doctor. Probably consisted of ground up insects and animal dung or something. "Well I—"

She raised her eyebrows and pointed a finger at him. "Don't say to me no. They're good for you."

He wouldn't dream of it. "Okay," he said with a grin. She was just so damn funny when she got all fierce. No wonder Carm had so much fire in her.

Mama Cruz narrowed her eyes at him. "You can't throw them away, either, because you just gave me your word you'd take them."

"Yes, ma'am." It was one bottle. He wouldn't die. Probably.

A happy smile curved her mouth and she patted his cheek. *"Te amo, mi hijo."*

He still didn't know much Spanish, but that he understood. "Love you too, Mama."

As she walked away pulling her rolling suitcase

behind her, he draped an arm around Carm's shoulders. The four of them stood there waving when Mama Cruz looked back from inside the terminal doors.

She looked like she was about to cry, as though the thought of leaving her grown babies behind was just too hard to face. But she braved it out, waved one last time and walked toward the check-in desks.

Once she was out of sight they all piled back into Ethan's truck. Sawyer slid into the back beside Carm and reached for her hand. She twined her fingers through his and laid her head back against the headrest, closing her eyes with a sigh. "Oh, God, I thought she'd never leave," she moaned.

Ethan chuckled from up front. "What, you didn't love living with her for the past two-and-a-half months?"

Carm opened her eyes to glare at her brother. "No. And thanks a lot for offering to have her for a few weeks to give us a break."

Marisol turned to face her from the shotgun seat. "I wanted to have her, to give you guys a break, but she wasn't having any of it."

"Don't worry about it," Carm said with a wave. "I'm just glad to have our space back." She closed her eyes again. "I'm so having a nap when we get home."

Sawyer perked up at that. Naps were awesome. Because when done together, they often led to even more pleasurable things. "I could totally go for a nap." And bonus, he and Carm could be as loud as they wanted in the bedroom now, because there was no one else at home to hear them. He loved it when Carm lost control, her moans and cries filling the room.

"Only a couple more months until she comes back for the wedding," Carm murmured, almost to herself. "You guys can split the hosting duties with us," she added to Ethan and Marisol.

"Hey, you could always elope and avoid all the

hassle," Ethan said as he merged onto the highway and headed back into town.

"Not gonna happen," she said. "But at least now it won't be nearly as big a production."

He wasn't sad about that.

Over the past several weeks Carm and her mom had scaled the wedding plans back drastically. Now it was going to be a small, intimate wedding with the ceremony taking place in the parish church Carm and her family had attended while growing up back in Miami. Also, instead of a lavish reception at some hotel with two hundred people to feed, it would be a catered dinner in Mama Cruz's backyard with just close family from her side, and Sawyer's teammates if they could make it.

Although he doubted Schroder would come. Doc had pulled away from everyone big time.

"It's a big relief, actually," Carm continued, breaking him out of his thoughts. "I was getting way too carried away before with everything. This will be so much better."

Sawyer had already told her he was fine with the original plan, but Carm had been adamant that this new arrangement was what she wanted. She'd told him the scare of nearly losing him had put everything into perspective, and she didn't want him to be uncomfortable on their wedding day. Seizing on his good luck, he'd just said thank you and kept his mouth shut after.

Carm covered a yawn with her hand. "When are we supposed to be at Tuck and Celida's again?"

The whole team had the week off and were going there for a cookout tonight. They needed to hang out and unwind together with everything that had happened. A few members of Gold Team might show up too. They'd stormed the cabin in Georgia the day after the crash, taking the male suspect into custody and safely getting the rest of the family out, including the dead teenage daughter. "Six, right?" he said to Ethan.

"Yeah. I'm bringing the beer. You guys are supposed to bring a dessert."

"Right." He shot Carm a wicked smile. "But it's okay if we're a little late."

She snorted a laugh. "I said nap. As in sleep."

He had total faith in his ability to change her mind, and planned to do just that.

"Is Schroder coming?"

At her question Sawyer glanced at Ethan. "You talked to him about it?"

At first when Doc had been sent home from the hospital, the entire team had taken turns going over to visit him. Bit by bit he'd withdrawn from them all, even DeLuca, until he'd finally flat out asked them not to come. Sawyer and the other guys still called him, but nothing they said lifted his spirits any. Tuck and Cruzie were the only two who kept going to see him, though Schroder made it plain he just wanted to be left alone.

"Talked to Taya this morning. She tried to convince him to come by even for fifteen minutes. No go." Ethan shook his head. "He's in a real bad spot right now. Taya's a bit better. It's helped a lot that all the women have been reaching out to her."

"Yeah." Sawyer couldn't imagine what his friend was going through. Losing your sight was a catastrophic blow that changed life completely. And Schroder and Taya had a baby on the way, too. "I wish I knew how the hell to help him."

"Yeah, I know," Ethan said in a voice heavy with regret. "We all do."

Chapter Thirteen

The sportscasters were offering an analysis about some play or other that had just happened in the football game.

Nate's favorite team was playing New England, but he wasn't even listening to the audio. Didn't give a shit about the game whatsoever as he sat in the leather recliner across from the TV in the living room. It was merely a habit he'd gotten into over the past few weeks, leaving the television going to fill the empty black void around him with sound so he didn't lose his mind.

He'd been home for almost seven weeks now. His incisions had all healed, his liver and lungs mostly recovered from the trauma he'd sustained, helped along by various meds and expensive hyperbaric chamber treatments covered by the Bureau. But the residual bruising and swelling in the occipital lobe of his brain that contained the visual cortex left him in continual darkness.

Adapting to his new reality was a constant struggle. He had more blah days now than bad or good ones, the headaches were improving. Usually he was able to fight back and conquer the monster of depression, but today…today was bad.

Despair had him pinned down. Day after day he sat here in this chair, carefully placed in this exact position by the occupational therapist who came every other day to work with him. Trying to get him adjusted to his new life.

One he fucking resented with every fiber of his being.

The sense of isolation was the hardest part of losing his vision. Taya was always around, never left him for longer than thirty or forty minutes at a time when she had to run out for groceries or to run errands. But even she couldn't lift the veil of blackness. Not even her love and support could pull him out of the darkness he'd sunk into, dragged down deeper and deeper until he didn't know how to claw his way out.

He was trying his best to keep his shit together but days like this he wished he'd died in the explosion instead of having to endure the probability of spending the rest of his life floundering this way. A tragedy caused by a damn drone, of all things.

The Bureau had found and charged a twenty-two-year-old engineering student for operating it inside a restricted area. Due to the severity of the incident, the kid would likely see jail time.

Nate felt no sympathy for him. Because of that fucking moron, people had died and he was goddamn *blind*.

His hands tightened on the armrests of the chair. The baby was due in another few months. How was he supposed to be a husband and father when he couldn't even take care of himself?

God, he *hated* feeling this way. The depression train he was riding had pulled away from the station and was rolling along the track, picking up steam with each passing mile. Nate didn't feel like fighting it today, so he let the chaotic thoughts in his mind continue.

He could barely feed himself, couldn't even shave his own face. Everything in their condo had been carefully positioned and was never to be moved so much as an inch so that he could memorize it all and navigate his way around with the damn cane he was forced to learn to use. There was no goddamn way he could help take care of a baby.

He'd never get to see his own child. That gutted him more than anything. He'd never see his or her face, never be able to watch a Christmas pageant or throw a ball with them.

Life as he'd known it was over, and what lay ahead was terrifying. His career was done. He'd never serve with the HRT again. How was he supposed to provide for his family if he couldn't fucking see?

He bit down on the inside of his cheek as mingled rage and despair suffocated him, filling his useless goddamn eyes with hot tears. Here he was, sitting on his ass like a fucking useless ornament, completely dependent on others to look after him. An adult child for Taya to have to take care of during what should have been the happiest time of her life while she prepared to fulfill her dream of becoming a mother.

Releasing a slow, shaky breath, he struggled to pull the chute on the gloomy freefall of depression he was trapped on. He felt bad for how he'd snapped at Taya when she'd tried to talk to him before leaving to run errands. Their marriage was suffering under the constant strain, their sex life practically nonexistent. It was testament to just how bad things had gotten that he rarely even wanted sex these days.

A cheer from the crowd in the background drew his attention back to the game on TV, reminding him of what day and time it was. Monday night.

The team was getting together again at Tuck and Celida's tonight. The third gathering he'd missed since the accident.

Since he'd come out of the coma the guys had all been great, trying to be there for him, but it killed Nate for any of them to see him this way. Helpless as a baby. Especially DeLuca, who was his idol.

Tuck had shown up last night and tried personally to convince Nate to come to the team function. Then Cruzie had called him this morning, trying to change his mind.

Not happening. Nate hadn't gone to any of the team functions since he'd left the hospital, and he wasn't going to this one either. Tuck and DeLuca had both told him that the guy who'd replaced him was only there on a temporary basis, and when Nate was cleared to come back, his spot would be waiting for him.

Bull. Shit.

He wasn't a part of the team anymore and would never be again. The last thing he wanted was to be an honorary mascot or an object of pity. Better for everyone if he withdrew now, distanced himself from all of them and learned to live without them.

His heightened sense of hearing picked up the muted sounds of a key scraping in the front door lock. He didn't turn his head toward it but he could feel Taya standing there in the entryway, watching him. Probably trying to judge what kind of mood he was in, figure out if it was safe to try and engage him in conversation.

That made him loathe himself even more.

"It's quarter after five," she said, the hesitance in her voice putting him close to tears again. Taya shouldn't have to walk on eggshells around him.

He didn't mean to take any of this out on her. He loved her. It was just… How could she love him if he was nothing but a burden to her? After everything she'd been through she deserved a hell of a lot more than that. In his darkest moments, Nate allowed himself to consider the possibility of her leaving him down the road. It wasn't fair for her to be saddled with him and his disability when she had a child to look after.

She cleared her throat. "The get together's at six. Matt and Sawyer both texted me. Everyone really wants to see you."

"I'm not going," he muttered.

Taya was quiet a moment. "Are you sure?"

"Yes." He bit back the angry words gathering at the back of his throat. None of this was her fault. Taya had been nothing but loving and protective since he'd been hurt, even shielding him from his sister and blocking her calls after her pathetic attempts to manipulate Taya while he was still in the induced coma.

"I was thinking I might go. Just for a little while, to visit."

It didn't surprise him that she wanted a break from his miserable ass. She'd done everything in her power to help and be there for him at every turn, and she deserved time to relax with friends. "Sure." Yet for some reason the thought of her going to a team function without him made something twist in his chest.

No. Going with her wouldn't make him feel any better, it would only make things worse, remind him of everything he'd lost. And it would make it harder when he pulled away again later. It had to be done, for his sanity.

She sighed, a tired, dispirited sound. "Okay. Are you hungry? I can make you something before I go."

"No, I'm good. Thanks," he added, although it didn't sound that polite.

"All right. I won't be long, an hour or two at most. Will you be okay?"

"Yeah." *I'm not okay. I'll never be okay again, and*

I don't know how to handle that.

Taya walked past him into their bedroom. When she came out a few minutes later he caught the scent of her perfume. Part of him wanted to grab her, haul her into his lap and just hold onto her as tight as he could. But that wasn't fair. She deserved some space.

He didn't want her to leave with this tension hanging between them, however. So he took a stab at making civil conversation, hoping to put them back on better terms. The private pity party had gone on long enough. "You were gone a while. Where did you go?"

"The doctor's."

At that he whipped his head around, facing in her direction even though he couldn't see her. "Why, what's wrong?"

She sighed. "Nothing's wrong, Nathan. I had my appointment with the OBGYN."

What? That had been today? Fuck. He'd been so wrapped up in himself, he'd totally forgotten. Now he felt awful. "Why didn't you say anything this morning?"

"Because you were being an asshole, and I was sick of you making everything about you, so I went on my own."

He flinched at the verbal slap, the palpable frustration in her voice. She'd never spoken like that to him before, so full of anger and resentment. But he deserved it. Every bit of it and more. He'd let her down so much, especially today. "God, Tay, I'm sorry."

She didn't answer.

Pushing to his feet, he reached for his cane and started toward her. He had to fix this, didn't blame her for being upset. He'd be utterly lost without her.

She deserved more support than he'd given her. Hell, she'd put the career she loved on hold to take care of him full time without a single complaint. While he'd been moping around feeling sorry for himself, she'd been handling everything on her own and he hadn't appreciated that the way he should have. God knew he hadn't put much effort into dealing productively with his situation.

His heart beat faster when he sensed her approaching him, meeting him halfway. It felt huge.

Reaching out a hand, his fingers met hers. He caught them, squeezed them tight as he reeled her in and wrapped both arms around her. "I'm sorry, baby." He meant it with every fiber of his being. Prayed she'd forgive him. "So damn sorry. And you're right, I've been an asshole. It's *not* all about me. I'm here for you too, and I'll do better from now on, I promise." Even though he couldn't see her he could feel her staring at him. Weighing his words and sincerity.

After a long moment, she slipped her arms around his waist. "Okay."

He exhaled a relieved breath and kissed the top of her head, almost dizzy. "What did the doc say?" Taya was what, around eighteen weeks or so now?

"We did an ultrasound."

His muscles locked tight. Christ, he couldn't believe he'd missed it. "Could she tell the gender?"

"Yes."

Nate swallowed. "Do you know what it is?" They hadn't really talked about whether they wanted to find out or not. He kind of wanted to know, but he'd respect her decision either way.

"Yes." She rubbed her cheek against his chest. "Do you want me to tell you?"

He couldn't stand the suspense. "Yes."

"It's a boy."

Nate squeezed his eyes shut as his throat locked up, the sudden knot of pride and awe there all but strangling him. "A boy." His eyes burned. They were having a son.

"And he's just beautiful, Nathan." Taya's voice was rough with emotion. "Perfectly formed, all his little organs functioning exactly as they should. I've got a picture of his little profile."

He couldn't speak. Couldn't find the words to express what he was feeling. *A son.* A little boy who would look up to him, depend on him, and needed his father to get his shit together in a hurry.

A gentle hand slid up the back of his neck to stroke his hair. "I know all this is hard on you," she murmured quietly after a moment. "But we still have so much to be grateful for."

Overwhelmed, he nodded, hugged her tighter. She was right. If this didn't snap him out of his funk, nothing would. He'd already lost his sight and career. He couldn't let the blindness take everything else from him. Couldn't let it destroy the rest of his life, especially his marriage and the chance to raise their son together. Taya was the best thing that had ever happened to him. "I love you so damn much," he choked out.

"I love you too. And so do your teammates. Don't push us away so hard."

He forced a nod, managed to hold it together. "I won't."

She took his face in her hands. "We need you, Nathan. All of us. And so does our son."

"I'll be there for you guys. Always." He'd learn braille. There were audio books and dictation software, and probably thousands of other things that would help him. His brain was fine. He could learn how to use a computer again. Look into what career options he still had. Maybe the Bureau had something he could still do.

Starting right now, he was giving himself a major attitude adjustment. By the time this baby was born, he was going to have his shit firmly together.

Loosening his hold, he eased back from Taya. He froze, then blinked. His heart stuttered. He swore he'd just seen a dim flicker of light in his peripheral vision, coming from where the living room window should be. Tiny dots, like pinpricks.

Taya shifted. "What is it?"

But no. He must have imagined it. All he saw was darkness. "Nothing."

She leaned up on tiptoe to press her lips to his. "I need to get going. Unless..." A loaded pause followed. "You want to come with me? Just for a little while."

The unspoken plea in her voice stopped the automatic denial before it could fly out of his mouth.

Actions spoke louder than words. He had to prove to her that he meant what he'd just said.

It was high time he faced this head on and came to terms with it. And he missed the guys like hell.

"Yeah," he said to her. "I'll go with you."

Chapter Fourteen

"I'm impressed. You changed that last diaper in twenty seconds flat," Taya said as she climbed out of the driver's seat of his truck.

Grinning, Nate got out of the passenger seat, shut his door and used his cane to follow her toward the elevator in their building's underground parking lot. He was getting the hang of it now. He'd been practicing a lot of things since finding out they were having a son a few days ago. "What can I say, I'm good with my hands."

"I can't argue with that. You should have seen the way Clay was watching you while you changed Libby. He was hovering over you the whole time, keeping an eagle eye on his baby girl even though you had her laid out flat on the floor." She chuckled. "Zoe just shook her head at him."

They'd gone over there for dinner, and so Nate could practice getting the hang of changing and dressing Libby. He felt way more confident now about his ability to help out with their son when he was born. "I don't blame him.

But at least she's big enough now that I'm not afraid I'll break her. When our little guy is born he's gonna be so tiny."

The team gathering the other night had gone well, better than he'd expected. The guys had been ecstatic to see him. Instead of pitying him or treating him like an invalid, they'd treated him exactly as they had before, trash talking and doling out shit like they always did. Nate had loved every moment of it. DeLuca had even promised to reach out to contacts on his behalf to see if there were any suitable openings in the Bureau for him.

"You'll be fantastic with him. Every time I imagine you holding him when he's born, I swear my heart will explode."

Nate smiled at that. His sense of touch was even more acute now than it had been before the accident. Something he'd been exploring with the help of Taya's naked body, to gratifying results. "I can't wait to hold him. I'm gonna be right in there during the delivery. I want to catch him and cut the cord. And I plan to rub that in Bauer's face so hard."

She snorted. "Why does this not surprise me. I swear you guys—"

Her words cut off so abruptly that he stopped dead, his muscles tensing. "Tay?" His body was on red alert, his remaining senses scanning for the threat.

"Hi, Nate. And you must be Taya."

The sound of that voice from over by the elevators sent a chill racing down his spine even as anger roared through him. *Dara.* "What are you doing here?" he demanded.

"I came to see you, make sure you were doing okay. I kept trying to find out, but nobody would return my calls."

No, because Taya had blocked her number back when he'd been in the coma, and Dara didn't have his contact info.

Nate clenched his jaw and stood his ground as he faced his sister, glad he couldn't see her. "How did you find me?"

"Really? That's how you react to me coming here?"

"Answer the question," he snapped. He caught the scent of Taya's perfume a second before her hand curled around his. Nate squeezed in reassurance, drew her into his side. He wasn't going to make this ugly. But he *was* going to make his stance absolutely clear.

"If you must know, I had to go through Taya's agent to get your address. I explained that I'm your sister and wanted to see you."

"Oh, shit," Taya whispered. Nate squeezed her hand again. It wasn't her fault. They would talk to the agent about it later.

"Well I don't want to see you," he shot back at Dara. "Pretty sure I made that plain the last time I did."

Dara huffed out an irritated breath. "We're family, Nate, like it or not."

No. The only family he had was standing right beside him, and the men who stood beside him on his team. "What do you want?"

"I told you, I came to see how you—"

"Cut the bullshit, Dara. You've got five seconds to answer me, and then I'm calling the cops because you're not welcome here and you know it."

Even though he couldn't see her, he could picture her glaring at him, a belligerent expression on a face almost identical to their dead mother's. "I think you know why."

Oh, I know *I know.* "You want my half of the inheritance."

Dara didn't respond, but she didn't have to.

"You tracked me down and came all the way here for less than two grand? Really?"

A tense pause answered him. "My finances are none

of your business. But not all of us have it as easy as you."

Easy.

Nate huffed out an ironic laugh. She thought he had it easy? "You're not getting the money. Not a single cent." It was already in an educational savings account for his son that he'd set up yesterday. To him it wouldn't have mattered if it was two thousand bucks or two cents.

The principle of it was the lesson here. This was about refusing to enable that sickening sense of entitlement Dara carried with her everywhere along with that giant chip on her shoulder. Like the world and everyone in it owed her something.

Nate didn't owe her shit.

"Look, I need that money a hell of a lot more than you do," she said, bitterness lacing every word.

Ah, she was in trouble again. Probably from racked up gambling debts or something like that. Not his problem. And even if he softened his stance and bailed her out this time, she'd just keep coming back for more. It would never end.

Oh, it's ending. It's ending here and now.

"The answer is no," he said flatly. "Now get out of here and don't come back. Ever. You show up again, you so much as try to contact either one of us again, and I'll slap a restraining order on your manipulative ass. You and I are done. Period. Am I clear?"

An ugly laugh answered him. "Fuck you, Nate."

No, fuck you. He didn't bother saying it. Thinking it was enough. He'd said all he had to say to her.

As her stomping footsteps on the concrete faded away in the distance, Nate stood where he was, his arm curled protectively around Taya's waist.

"Okay, she's gone," Taya said softly, then rubbed a hand over his lower back. "Are you all right?"

"I'm fine." Surprisingly fine. In the past any interaction with her had left him stewing and upset for hours, even days. Now he just felt a sense of finality. Maybe he'd file a restraining order anyway, just to ensure she wouldn't think about disrupting their life again at some point in the future.

"I'll phone my agent as soon as we get upstairs. I'm sorry, I can't believe she would give our address to anyone."

"Not your fault. Dara has a way of working people until she gets what she wants."

"Well she won't try it again with you. Not after this."

"Nope." Raising their joined hands to his mouth, he kissed the back of hers and started for the elevators.

She dialed her agent as soon as they reached their door. Going by memory and feel, he tapped the cane around to help him navigate his way back toward the master bedroom.

A few steps away from where the doorway should be, he stopped suddenly. Blinked. Blinked again.

Those spots again. Tiny dancing pinpricks of light in his peripheral vision.

It had happened a couple times before, and it always made his heart pound, always made him hope that maybe…

But no. His eyes looked straight toward the spot and saw only blackness.

Rather than allowing the crushing disappointment to take hold, he accepted it and moved on. Tired but strangely at peace after the altercation, he shuffled his way into their bedroom without bumping into a single thing, then stripped and got between the covers. Taya was still on the phone out in the kitchen. The sound of her voice soothed him, lulled him to sleep.

He jerked awake sometime later when a gasp broke the quiet. Taya was beside him, he could smell her sweet scent. Groggy, he rolled over, the cobwebs of sleep tangling his brain.

Then she bolted upright and sucked in a breath.

Alarm streaked through him and he shot up into a sitting position. "What's wrong?" he demanded, reaching for her.

"It's the baby."

Ice slid through him. Shit, had something happened to it? He felt so goddamn helpless, unable to see, to help. "What do you mean?" He ran through a list of possible complications she might be experiencing, none of them good. "Does something hurt? Are you bleeding?"

She giggled and grabbed his hand to press it to the mound of her belly. "No. It moved. I felt it. Like tiny bubbles popping inside me. It tickles." The awe in her voice made his heart clench. She pressed harder on his hand. "There, do you feel it?"

He paused, waiting, trying to detect the tiny movement beneath his palm with his heightened sense of touch. He wanted to, but… "No." She was almost nineteen weeks along. Exactly in the right timeframe to feel the baby moving. God, how incredible was that? Another reminder of how much he had to look forward to and live for.

"It's so amazing," she whispered, pressing his hand harder against her abdomen. "Our son, Nathan."

"Yeah." He rubbed his hand over the small swell, craving the contact. "Wish I could feel him."

"You will soon enough. And now that he's woken me up in the middle of the night, I have to pee," she muttered, and rolled away from him onto her hip. A second later the bedside light switch snapped on.

The black movie screen in front of him turned to dark gray.

Nate went dead still for a second, then rolled over and squinted at the faint light coming from the other side of the bed.

The *light*.

Taya froze. "Nathan? What's wrong?" She grabbed for his hand. "Is it another headache? Do your eyes hurt?"

Heart pounding, he blinked, squinted harder, thought he was either dreaming or that his mind was playing a cruel trick on him. But no, those were definitely lights and shadows he was seeing. And the blurry outline of his wife, her deep brown curls a fuzzy halo around her head.

"What?" she whispered in a stricken voice.

"I can see you," he choked out. "Tay, I can *see* you." The outline of her anyway, but that in itself was incredible and gave him an aching sense of hope. Was his sight coming back? Even blurry shapes and shadows were better than a world of eternal darkness.

Taya cried out and flung her arms around him, burying her face in his neck. "Oh, Nathan." Nate held her tight, overwhelmed by a flood of relief and gratitude. "We need to phone your neurologist."

"What time is it?"

"Two in the morning."

"No, let's wait a while yet."

"Is the light hurting your eyes? I can turn it off—"

"No." He stopped her, drawing her down beside him where he lay staring at her face. It was inches from his own, but he could make out the dark lines of her eyebrows and the shape of her mouth.

He slid a hand into her hair and kissed her. Kissed her again and again and again before lowering his head to the pillow, facing her. "Leave it on. I want to stare at you for the rest of the night."

The sight of her lips curving into a smile filled his chest with a gratitude that made him want to weep.

His vision *would* return. He just had to be patient. This was a fight he had to win.

With his little warrior by his side and their child on the way, he was going to beat the odds and regain his sight. He wouldn't accept any other option.

Chapter Fifteen

"Nathan, we can't. We don't have time, we need to leave here in fifteen minutes."

Nate ignored Taya's half-hearted, breathy protest and gripped her splayed thighs tighter in his hands, pulling her down to his waiting mouth. He savored his victory as she gasped then sighed in pleasure, wrapping her fingers around the top of the hotel headboard as she let her head fall back.

His timing had been perfect, catching her in the bathroom a few minutes ago while she was pulling her blue and white dress over her adorable baby bump. Before she'd managed to put on panties. He was sneaky like that.

He took full advantage of that easy access now, licking and stroking and sucking, teasing the swollen bud of her clit until she was writhing and mewling above him. She was in the third trimester now, and everything was going great. Especially the sex.

Her breasts were fuller now, her body twice as sensitive as normal from the extra blood volume she carried. She was also horny all the time these days, an unexpected symptom he was thrilled about. They'd had more sex in the past eight days than they'd had in the past six months combined. He could make her come so easily now, and much faster than normal. Sometimes more than once in a row. He freaking loved it. Wished she could stay pregnant forever.

But the absolute best part was being able to *see* her while he did.

That was something he'd never take for granted again. His vision had only completely returned to normal a couple weeks ago, and he was savoring every moment of it. Like right now, watching his gorgeous wife unravel for him.

Sucking gently on her clit, one hand creeping up to dip inside the bodice of her dress and cup the full curve of her breast to squeeze her hardened nipple, Nate gazed up at her, need and arousal humming through his entire body. Taya's mouth was open in a soft, sexy groan, eyes closed, all those glorious dark curls cascading over her shoulders as her thighs quivered on either side of his head.

"Put your fingers in me," she panted, arching her back, reaching down to grab the back of his head with one hand.

He'd do better than that. He was so damn hard it was a wonder he didn't bust the zipper on his dress pants.

Wrenching them and his underwear partway down his thighs, he curled his hands around her hips and eased her away from his mouth. She groaned in protest, but quickly shimmied down the length of his body and straddled his hips, his aching cock nestled against the soft, tender folds he'd just been enjoying.

Taya's gray eyes glowed with arousal, her cheeks flushed with it. She sat up taller, stripped the dress off over her head and tossed it aside, every motion of her hips a sweet torture.

But in spite of their tight timeline, she wasn't done tormenting him yet.

Poised there above him, she held his gaze, licked her lower lip as she reached back to undo her bra. He groaned like a man in delirium when her full breasts spilled free, the taut, darkened nipples begging for his attention. Nate cupped them reverently in his hands, tweaked the sensitive peaks with his thumbs before half-sitting up to capture one in his mouth.

Taya sucked in a sharp breath and cupped the back of his head, whimpering as she began to rock her slick folds up and down the length of his cock. God yeah, so sensitive and responsive to every intimate touch.

His head swam, her sweet scent twining around him, heart racing as though he'd just run ten miles. He wrapped an arm around her waist, firmly anchoring her to him. She reached down between them, curled her fingers around his throbbing length. He flicked his tongue across her nipple as he sucked it, moaned as she stood him up and began to sink down on him, enveloping him in her soft heat.

Nate squeezed his eyes shut and leaned back, pulling her with him. With one hand on her hip he helped her with the slow, hypnotic motion, each silky glide of her slick core along his length spreading pleasure up his spine. The position was slightly awkward with the bulk of her tummy in the way but she didn't seem to care. She moaned his name and rode him slowly, reaching one hand between her legs to play with her clit.

Nate switched breasts, his heart rate unsteady as her moans turned to panting breaths that signaled she was close to exploding. He managed to force his heavy eyelids open and look up into her face as she started to come, the sensual agony on her face destroying him.

She clenched around him, her fingers digging into his scalp while she cried out her pleasure, the pulses along his cock setting him off. With a harsh groan, he thrust up into her warmth and locked her to him with the hand on her hip, ecstasy bursting through his whole body.

After a long moment Taya slumped and rolled off him, lying on her side facing him. She pushed a tangled curl away from her eyes. "Now I need another shower but I don't have time." Her expression was playfully accusing, but her breathless tone and the glow of pleasure in her eyes told him she'd loved it just as much as him.

"Good. Now you'll smell like me the entire day."

She wrinkled her nose. "That's so caveman."

"Totally caveman," he agreed, snagging her around the waist and drawing her close for a kiss. "We'd better get ready. Don't wanna be late to the wedding."

Taya snorted and rolled away to find her dress. Seven minutes later they were in the rental car heading for the Miami church where Cruzie, his mom and sister had attended since they were kids.

They made it with three minutes to spare. Holding Taya's hand, Nate walked up the front steps to where the rest of the guys stood all decked out in their suits. "Is this a wedding, or a monkey suit convention for male FBI agent models?" he asked.

"Well if it isn't Dr. Feelgood," Cruzie, who was best man, said, grinning as he stepped forward to grab Nate in a hug. "Good to see you, man."

"Good to see you guys too. Believe me."

Everyone chuckled and Nate went to the groom next. Vance stood in parade rest posture in his tux, broad shoulders straight, feet braced apart and hands clasped behind his back. He was missing his trademark Stetson, in deference to the church ceremony. Nate had no doubt he'd have it back on for the reception though.

"Hey, man. You nervous?" Nate asked.

A big, bright grin split his dark face. "Nope. Not even a little."

"Glad to hear it." He and Carm were a great match,

and he and Cruzie were already brothers in every way that mattered. The marriage would just make it official. "Congrats again, man." Nate reeled him in for a hard, back-slapping man hug.

As soon as he stepped back Bauer was there, waiting to smack Nate on the shoulder with a solid fist. "So, this mean you're back now? Tuck said you would be soon."

"Yes and no." Tuck and Cruzie had spent the most time with him during his recovery, but the entire team had been awesome with him. He'd gone to every team function since the day he'd made the decision to flip the switch. They were one big, solid, pain-in-the-ass family again.

He loved each and every one of these guys like brothers.

"Few more weeks off, then hopefully a clean CT scan and they'll clear me to resume active duty." He'd been working out with the guys and going with them to the shooting range for the past three weeks or so, but nothing seriously strenuous or anything that would cause another knock to the head. Nate didn't want anything to set his recovery back. He'd been off way too long already and was itching to get back to work with the team.

"Awesome." Bauer grabbed him around the shoulders with one huge arm and scrubbed his knuckles over Nate's hair hard enough to burn his scalp. "Didn't think I'd miss having you around so much, Doc."

Nate huffed out a laugh. "Aww, that's sweet. I missed you too, Bauer. And why the hell are you in such a good mood, anyway?"

Bauer released him. "Libby's at home with my mom looking after her. So Zoe and I are here alone." He raised his eyebrows, letting the weight of that sink in a minute for Nate. "We got seven hours of uninterrupted sleep last night. Seven," he said, as if it was the most miraculous thing that had ever happened to him.

"Yeah, right. Sleep," Nate said with a sarcastic chuckle.

Bauer lowered his eyebrows. "No, I'm serious. We slept. All night, without waking up once. It was amazing."

"That's pathetic, man. I mean really, truly pitiful. I'm sad for you. And for Zoe."

Bauer smirked at him. "Yeah, let's revisit this conversation again in another four or five months. Then we'll see who's laughing."

"Okay, people, let's get inside before the bride shows up," Tuck ordered with a clap of his hands. "All the other hot ladies are already inside," he said to Taya with a smile.

Nate took her hand, tucked it into the crook of his arm and led her through the doors of the old Catholic church. She shot him a secret little smile, her cheeks pink.

"What?" he asked.

She leaned into his shoulder. "Nothing. Just happy."

He smiled back. He just loved her to pieces. "Good."

She nodded, faced the altar at the far end of the aisle. "Mmm. *Feel* good, too." She dropped her voice to a whisper, leaned toward him slightly so that only he could hear her, the curve of her breast rubbing against his arm.

Nate's gaze dipped down to her cleavage. That brush hadn't seemed like an accident. And he could see the outline of her nipples pressing against her dress. Wait, was she turned on? There was something in her tone that made him think wicked thoughts, but he had to be wrong, they were in a church and his wife was pretty proper about that kind of stuff.

"Yeah?" He dragged his eyes back to her face, studied her.

One side of her mouth quirked, as if she was trying not to smile. "A little *too* good," she added, slanting him a naughty look.

His brain stuttered. Nate almost stumbled there in the aisle as he realized what was going on. His wife was horny again. Already.

Taya bit her bottom lip, that hungry gleam in her eyes making him want to lean down and nibble on it himself. "I can't stop thinking about earlier. How many hours before we can do a repeat?"

She was doing this to him now? Here? "Too long," he muttered, resuming his pace. "Way too damn long." He smothered a laugh at Taya's disappointed groan.

Medically speaking, her pregnancy was progressing perfectly. He wasn't the one dealing with constant heartburn and backache and the baby keeping her up all night with its kicking, but this supercharged libido of hers was an awesome and unexpected bonus he planned to enjoy to the fullest for as long as it lasted. "And you felt the need to torture me like this because?"

Taya shrugged, a slight smirk twisting her mouth. "Because I didn't want to suffer alone. And now you'll be looking forward to it for the rest of the day."

Christ yeah, he would. He'd barely be able to think about anything else. Jesus.

He escorted her to their pew where the team was waiting. God, now he was hard in the middle of a freaking church, the evidence of his arousal shoved right up there against the front of his pants for everyone to see. He might as well have a neon sign across his forehead. *Hey, check out my raging hard on in the middle of this church!*

Taya slid along the pew bench toward the others. Bauer scooted closer to Zoe and cocked an eyebrow at him. "What were you two whispering about back there?"

"Nothing." He sat, quickly put his hands in his lap. *Down, boy. Down, damn you.*

Taya reached over and took his hand, her fingers briefly curling around his erection through his dress pants, the contact nearly making him choke. He gripped her hand and shot her a warning glance, but she was facing forward, her expression all innocence.

Innocent, his ass. His wife was a total wanton, seemed to walk around in a constant state of arousal these days.

How freaking lucky could one man get?

Without turning his head, Nate studied her out of the corner of his eye. The afternoon sunlight streamed through the tall stained glass windows on the right side of the church, covering her with rainbows. The mother of his child, and what a lucky baby their son was because of that.

She was so damn beautiful it almost hurt to look at her.

Almost.

But the difference now compared to before the accident was that he made sure to appreciate each and every color reflected on her skin and hair, illuminating her like the angel she was.

An angel he planned to pin to the bed and take straight to heaven and back the moment they set foot in their hotel room tonight.

—The End—

Thank you for reading SHATTERED. I really hope you enjoyed it and that you'll consider leaving a review at one of your favorite online retailers. It's a great way to help other readers discover new books.

If you liked SHATTERED and would like to read more, turn the page for a list of my other books. And if you don't want to miss any future releases, please feel free to join my newsletter:

http://kayleacross.com/v2/newsletter/

Complete Booklist

ROMANTIC SUSPENSE

DEA FAST Series
Falling Fast
Fast Kill
Stand Fast
Strike Fast

Colebrook Siblings Trilogy
Brody's Vow
Wyatt's Stand
Easton's Claim

Hostage Rescue Team Series
Marked
Targeted
Hunted
Disavowed
Avenged
Exposed
Seized
Wanted
Betrayed
Reclaimed
Shattered

Titanium Security Series
Ignited
Singed
Burned
Extinguished
Rekindled
Blindsided: A Titanium Christmas novella

Bagram Special Ops Series
Deadly Descent
Tactical Strike
Lethal Pursuit
Danger Close
Collateral Damage
Never Surrender (a MacKenzie Family novella)

Suspense Series
Out of Her League
Cover of Darkness
No Turning Back
Relentless
Absolution

PARANORMAL ROMANCE
Empowered Series
Darkest Caress

HISTORICAL ROMANCE
The Vacant Chair

EROTIC ROMANCE (writing as ***Callie Croix***)
Deacon's Touch
Dillon's Claim
No Holds Barred
Touch Me
Let Me In
Covert Seduction

About the Author

NY Times and USA Today Bestselling author Kaylea Cross writes edge-of-your-seat military romantic suspense. Her work has won many awards and has been nominated for both the Daphne du Maurier and the National Readers' Choice Awards. A Registered Massage Therapist by trade, Kaylea is also an avid gardener, artist, Civil War buff, Special Ops aficionado, belly dance enthusiast and former nationally-carded softball pitcher. She lives in Vancouver, BC with her husband and family.

You can visit Kaylea at www.kayleacross.com. If you would like to be notified of future releases, please join her newsletter: http://kayleacross.com/v2/newsletter/

Manufactured by Amazon.ca
Acheson, AB